*NANCY DREW AND THE HARDY BOYS
TEAM UP—WHEN A CRUISE SHIP
BECOMES THE DEATH BOAT . . .*

Nancy swam underwater the length of the pool until she came up for air just inches from Frank's face.

He was swimming facedown, not moving.

"Frank Hardy, you can't fool me with that dead man's float." Nancy laughed. "Frank? Frank?"

"Yes, Nancy, I'm right here. How's the water?" Frank asked from the deck of the pool.

Nancy froze, and her heart started thumping a thousand times a minute.

It wasn't Frank Hardy in the pool with her. It was someone else—and he was dead!

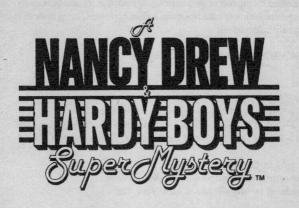

# A NANCY DREW & HARDY BOYS Super Mystery ™

## DOUBLE CROSSING

### Carolyn Keene

**AN ARCHWAY PAPERBACK**
Published by POCKET BOOKS
New York    London    Toronto    Sydney    Tokyo

AN ARCHWAY PAPERBACK *Original*

An Archway Paperback published by
POCKET BOOKS, a division of Simon & Schuster Inc.
1230 Avenue of the Americas, New York, N.Y. 10020

ISBN: 0-671-64917-5

First Archway Paperback printing June 1988

10  9  8  7  6  5  4  3  2

Printed in the U.S.A.

IL 7+

# DOUBLE CROSSING

# Chapter

## One

"FRANK HARDY! What are *you* doing here?"

Nancy Drew looked up at the young man's handsome face with an inquiring smile. She hadn't seen her friend in ages, and here they were, bumping into each other on the deck of a luxury cruise ship. "This is truly incredible." Nancy laughed.

The offshore breeze was whipping her reddish blond hair across her face, so Nancy set her luggage on the deck and tucked the unruly strands behind her ears. Just then a group of passengers slowly filed by them, checking out the ship and talking quietly.

1

Frank gave her a friendly but distant look. "I think you're mistaking me for someone else," he said politely.

Nancy looked at him again. He was about six feet tall, lean, and muscular. An expensive camera dangled around his neck, and he was wearing a blue and white T-shirt with a picture of the cruise ship they were on—the S.S. *Duchess.* A small plastic tag pinned to his shirt read Crew Member.

Still, that smiling face was *definitely* Frank Hardy's. It wasn't the kind of face any girl could forget.

Nancy glanced into Frank's deep brown eyes again. This time she caught a wink.

"Oh. Sorry," she murmured coolly. "You really do look *exactly* like someone I went to high school with. By the way, my name is Nancy Drew. My girlfriend George Fayne is the assistant social director on this cruise. Perhaps you know her."

"Well, you've got the first name right, anyway. I'm Frank Bresson, the ship's photographer." Frank extended his hand and squeezed hers warmly. "Nice to meet you, Nancy."

Behind them, the crowd had scattered. Nancy looked around and saw that they were alone. "What's going on, Frank?" she asked softly.

Frank's eyes darted around the deck and he nodded his head toward one of the halls leading off it. Nancy followed him down the hall.

"The captain of this ship hired Joe and me to work undercover. Joe's a busboy in the dining room—would you believe it? He doesn't seem to mind. There are lots of pretty waitresses for him to hang out with."

Nancy laughed. Frank's younger brother, Joe, was a notorious flirt. "Same old Joe, huh?" she said.

"Same old Joe."

"How's Callie?" Callie Shaw was Frank's longtime girlfriend.

"She's great. She—"

Frank was about to say more, when the elevator doors opened behind them and a crowd got out. There were a party of elderly women and a few staff personnel. Nancy watched as Frank scanned the group.

Then, just as the elevator doors were closing, a group of five young people about Nancy and Frank's age, eighteen or so, came up behind them.

"Rats—we missed it," muttered a thin, blond-haired girl. She pressed the call button repeatedly.

The five were obviously together—two girls and three guys. They were laughing and jos-

3

tling one another, but when they noticed Nancy and Frank, they stopped fooling around and stood in silence.

Well, thought Nancy. Might as well make friends. We're all going to be spending five days on the same boat. "Hi, there," she said with a smile.

She was greeted with five stony stares.

"How's it going?" Frank asked, trying to lighten the atmosphere.

"Didn't your mother ever tell you not to talk to strangers?" the blond girl asked sarcastically, glaring at Frank.

The look of surprise on Frank's face flashed on like a neon light and then quickly flashed off again. Wonder what I did to set her off, he thought. But all he said was, "Sorry, just doing my job."

The five friends stared at the camera hanging around Frank's neck. Then one of the guys—the one with glasses and a university sweatshirt—held up a make-believe camera to his face and pretended to snap Frank's picture. The others all giggled.

"Come on, let's take the stairs," a blond guy suggested. "Leave the guy alone, Connor. You heard him—he's only doing his job."

"Yeah, okay," the others said.

They all moved away from the elevator at

the same time. Frank and Nancy stared after them as they headed for the companionway.

"Talk about an attitude problem," Frank said when the five kids were gone and he and Nancy were alone again.

Just then, another passenger appeared in the hallway. Nancy and Frank turned away from each other and pretended to be strangers waiting for the elevator.

When the passenger had passed them, Nancy leaned toward Frank. "I'm staying with my friend," she whispered, to let him know where to contact her.

"Oh, yes. The assistant social director. I saw her name on the ship's log when I signed on today. She's in Cabin Thirty-seven, I believe," Frank whispered back. Then, in a louder voice, he added, "Well, have a good trip, miss."

A moment later the elevator doors opened again, and Frank got on with a secret wave and a wink.

Nancy turned away from the elevator as the public address system came to life. "Ladies and gentlemen, welcome aboard the *Duchess,*" a gruff but friendly voice said. "This is Captain Helgesen speaking. We're off on a five-day Caribbean Sea cruise from Miami to Cozumel, Mexico, home of the ancient Mayan ruins. We hope you have a pleasant journey, and please remember, we're here to serve you! Bon voyage!"

Nancy threaded her way back to her luggage, through the passengers who were coming on board, curious about what Frank Hardy had said. Frank and Joe were excellent detectives, with many tough cases to their credit. Their dad was a well-known private investigator and a super sleuth himself. If the Hardys were on a case, that meant there was trouble on board the *Duchess*.

But then, Nancy had to remind herself, *she* was there to have fun in the sun. And this time she'd leave the detecting to the Hardys and concentrate on relaxing. That's why George had invited her, and that's just what she intended to do. Still, she couldn't help being a little curious about what the Hardy brothers were up to.

"Cabin number thirty-seven," Nancy said to herself as she walked down the hall, checking the numbers on the door. She pulled the door to number thirty-seven open and set her luggage down on the lower bunk. The room was tiny but spotless, and the bright white of the walls made it seem larger than it really was. Colorful plaid bedspreads added a cheerful note.

On the pillow of her bed Nancy saw a note from George welcoming her aboard. In it she told Nancy to meet her on the Crown Deck, where she was working.

Nancy unpacked quickly, pulling a card from Ned Nickerson out of her purse and putting it on top of her bureau, where she could look at it. She read it once again.

"My Dear Ms. Detective," it said. "While you're sailing off into the sunset, how am I supposed to solve a not-so-mysterious case of loneliness? Miss you, and see you when you get home. Love, Ned."

What a guy. Ned Nickerson had to be the greatest boyfriend a girl ever had or ever could have. Nancy promised herself that no matter how good-looking the guys were on this cruise, she wasn't even going to *think* about romance.

And *especially* not with Frank Hardy. She'd crossed paths with Frank and his brother before, and every time she did, Frank had the same powerful effect on her. Nothing had ever happened between them, though, and it wasn't going to this time, either. She had a boyfriend, he had a girlfriend—and that was that.

Nancy quickly changed out of the clothes she was wearing into a more casual outfit.

"Now to see George," she said, checking herself out in the mirror. The starched white shorts and bold red-and-white-striped cotton sweater were perfect.

So long, Nancy Drew, detective, she

thought, making her way out of her cabin and up to the Crown Deck. Nancy Drew, luxury-cruise passenger, is all ready for the sailing party to begin!

At the railing on the Crown Deck, Nancy watched a crowd of passengers toss confetti and streamers down onto the well-wishers below as the crew took up the gangplank.

"Hey, Nancy!" shouted a voice from behind.

Nancy turned and saw her friend George Fayne rushing toward her with open arms. George was the perfect example of all four of the summer Ts—tall, tan, thin, and terrific. Her dark hair was cut short, and her sun-bronzed skin looked fabulous against a short white skirt and blue T-shirt. The T-shirt was just like Frank's—it said S.S. *Duchess* Crew Member, in white letters.

The two friends gave each other a big hug as a greeting.

"I can't believe I haven't seen you for two whole months," Nancy said. "How's the job going?"

"It's great!" said George. "I mean, think about it: three Olympic-size swimming pools, a gym and health spa, a sauna, plus tennis, volleyball, even archery and skeet shooting. I'm in heaven!"

"I can tell," Nancy said. "But—" She was interrupted by the long, low, and deafening sound of the ship's foghorn. The ship was pulling out of port now, away from Miami's shore. The crowd of well-wishers at the dock was growing smaller and smaller.

"Uh-oh—got to run," George yelled, trying to be heard above the powerful horn. "That's my cue to get down to the Princess Deck and start the social activities. We'll talk tonight, after the scavenger hunt, okay?"

"Sure," Nancy agreed as George started to dash off. Then she suddenly caught George by the arm. "Oh, George, wait!" Nancy lowered her voice. "Did you know that Frank and Joe Hardy are on board as crew members?"

"You're kidding! They must have just signed on, because I run into *everybody*," George reported.

"They're on a case, so don't blow their cover," Nancy said. "They're not even supposed to be brothers."

"Got it," George called as she slipped away through the crowd. "I never saw them before in my life."

"May I have your attention, ladies and gentlemen?" George was standing in the front of the enormous dining room, a microphone in her hand.

"I'd like to explain the rules of tonight's scavenger hunt. To start: the color of your napkin will decide which team you're on."

"I must be on the cherries-jubilee-stain team!" someone shouted, and everyone roared with laughter.

As George spoke, Nancy's eyes wandered around the huge room, taking in the beautifully dressed cruise passengers, who were talking and laughing at their tables.

She spotted Joe Hardy not far from her, busily clearing dessert dishes from a table. Blond-haired, blue-eyed Joe had a smile for everyone, but especially for everyone female. Balancing dishes in a precarious stack, he joked with a group of giggling girls, "Hey, you hardly touched those eclairs. Remember, there's no such thing as a diet on this ship."

The girls blushed and giggled even more. Nancy smiled with amusement. Joe Hardy really knew how to flirt.

As Joe approached Nancy's table, she whispered to him, "You're going to do great on tips this week, Joe."

Joe winked. "Nancy! Hi!" he said softly so no one else could hear. "Did Frank tell you about the case we're on?"

Nancy shook her head. "No. And I'm dying of curiosity. Maybe I can help you solve it."

"Never mind," Joe said with a laugh.

"We've got our reputation to protect. Can't have you making us look bad."

"No chance of that," said Nancy. "But I guess it's just as well. I'm here on vacation. I was curious, though—"

"Better watch that stuff, Drew," Joe teased. "It killed a cat once, or so I heard."

Suddenly Nancy's full attention was directed back to George. "And if your napkin is yellow," George was saying, "you're in luck. You have an ace detective on your team. Her name is Nancy Drew—and she happens to be my best friend!" George announced proudly, pointing to Nancy.

"Oh, great, George," Nancy murmured under her breath as she nodded to the crowd. "Now everyone knows I'm a detective."

Joe shook his head with a smile. "I'd better get out of here before she blows *my* cover. See you later, Nancy."

"You've got five minutes to meet and divide up your lists before the scavenger hunt begins," George said. "First team to bring back everything on its list wins."

Nancy looked over the list George handed her. An ashtray from the ship's discotheque. A wet towel from the men's locker room. A queen of hearts card from the ship's gambling casino—and those were the *easy* ones. Then there was a tear-stained love letter, a raw onion, a massage (how was she going to get that?), a hot water bottle, a wilted flower, and more. There were twenty things in all on her team's list.

After her team met, they split up, and Nancy's first assignment was to go up to the Palace Deck to find a tie line from a life preserver. This sure beats real detecting, she thought to herself.

The calm sea and quiet, breezeless night were beautiful in the moonlight. Nancy paused under a metal-grating stairway to gaze at the light shimmering and dancing on the water and half imagined that it smiled back at her. Dear Ned, she thought to herself, composing an imaginary letter. If only you were here . . .

Footsteps on the stairs above her interrupted her thoughts. First there was the squeak of rubber soles. Then the tap of leather heels. "Hi," she heard a woman say softly.

"Hello," a man replied in an accented voice.

Ah, yes, Nancy thought with a smile. Cruise magic. They had probably met just a few hours ago. . . . Maybe they had found this dark stairway to meet for a kiss. . . . Nancy didn't want to chase them away, so she remained perfectly still, hidden below them.

"I see your shopping bag is from Plummer's," said the man. His accent was definitely Spanish.

"That's what it says," the girl replied nervously. Her voice was American, and she sounded young.

"Then you are Pipeline?" he asked.

"Yes," said the girl.

What in the world was going on? Not exactly romance, Nancy thought.

"And tell me, what precisely is on these disks?" the man asked.

"I've already told you—codes, maps, covert operation plans—everything."

They were both quiet for a moment. Finally the man asked another question. "Your father works for the CIA—that is how you got this information?"

Craning her neck, Nancy tried to look through the small grating holes of the stairs. She couldn't see the girl, and all she could see of the man were white trouser cuffs and white shoes. They had to be from a ship's uniform, she realized.

"Yeah, he works for the CIA. That's what I said," the girl answered. Then she got angry. "Look, I don't want to play Twenty Questions. Take this. It's the sample disk you wanted. If you like what you see, meet me tomorrow morning at six on the Princess Deck. And don't forget to bring the money."

Nancy couldn't believe what she was hearing. Someone was selling a computer disk full of CIA secrets! She had to find out who they were and stop them.

Just then, a man's strong arms reached out and grabbed Nancy by the shoulders—not harshly but forcefully. Was he trying to keep her from following the two people on the stairs?

"Hey!" Nancy's cry of surprise was cut off as his arms went around her back, drawing her to him. Then his warm lips were pressing hers in a dizzying kiss as the footsteps on the stairs sped up and began to run.

They were getting away!

# Chapter

## Two

"Let me go!" Nancy tried to say to the guy who was holding her close. But all that came out was "Mmmnphff." His lips were still pressed to hers, and the two people above them were escaping!

Finally Nancy jabbed his stomach with her elbow. Stunned, he let go abruptly.

"Sorry," said Nancy, running up the metal stairs as fast as she could.

"Hey, wait a minute," the phantom kisser shouted, following her.

The stairs led to a large, open deck with shuffleboard courts. Along one wall was a row of deck chairs facing the outside railing. But at this hour the chairs were all empty, and the place was deserted.

Nancy yanked open a door that led to a pair of elevators. The lights above them indicated that they were both going down.

They got away! Nancy decided in frustration. If only she'd been quicker, she might at least have gotten a look at their faces.

When she returned to the deserted moonlit deck, the tall stranger was waiting.

"Hey, you didn't have to run away like that," he said, sounding embarrassed. "I wasn't going to hurt you."

Nancy looked at the phantom kisser, taking him in for the first time. He was one of the boys that she'd seen by the elevator earlier that day—the tall blond one who had told the others to lay off Frank, in fact. He had an open look, with friendly green eyes and a dimpled grin. All in all, his was a nice face, a very nice face, and Nancy couldn't help liking him. "I wasn't running from you," she said. "Though I didn't exactly appreciate being grabbed!"

"I want to explain," he said tentatively.

"Okay. Let's hear it," said Nancy, her arms crossed over her chest.

"Well," he murmured, and then stopped. Obviously this guy was more confident with his kisses than with his words. "Well, for one thing, I don't usually go around kissing girls I've never met—"

"Oh. But you made an exception in my case?" asked Nancy with a wry grin. "Thanks a lot."

"No, no," he said, smiling and rubbing his chin with the back of his hand. "It was a game! Part of the scavenger hunt. I was supposed to get a kiss from a beautiful stranger. I came up here, and when I saw you standing in the moonlight, I said to myself—now, *there* is a beautiful stranger. I'm awfully sorry if I offended you—"

He kept looking at Nancy as if he were afraid she'd be angry with him.

"You're traveling with four friends, aren't you?" Nancy said.

"Yes! How did you know?"

"I saw you earlier by the elevator. I was standing with the ship's photographer," she explained.

"Of course! I thought you looked familiar. My name is David Carlyle." He grinned and offered his hand.

"Hi, David," Nancy said. She put out her hand and shook his. "Your friends weren't very friendly today, by the way."

"Sorry about that. I guess some of us are a little spoiled. We're all diplomats' kids."

Diplomats' kids—there was an interesting

17

phrase. Nancy's lawyer father, Carson Drew, had told her once that *diplomat* could be a code word for the CIA.

Nancy was silent, remembering what she had just overheard under the stairs. "Your father works for the CIA," the man with the accent had said. A coincidence? Nancy had stopped believing in coincidences many cases ago.

"Well, so far," David said, "I know that you're a great kisser and a very understanding person. Do I get to know your name?"

"Nancy. Nancy Drew."

"Oh, you're the detective. Hi, Nancy. Well, can I help you find anything on your list? That's the least I can do, since you helped me."

Nancy thought that maybe he could help her—but later. "No, thanks. I'd better be getting back," she said. "See you around."

Nancy turned and hurried straight to the ballroom to find George and the Hardys.

She had to zigzag her way through the scavenger hunt dancers on the large ballroom floor to get to George, who was sitting behind the judges' table. Glints of light from the enormous glass chandelier shimmered on the walls and over the dancing couples.

"Nancy," George scolded, "where's your tie line?"

"I forgot it," Nancy said. She leaned over

and whispered urgently in George's ear. "Tell Frank I've got to see him. Something very strange is happening on this boat."

"Hi," David said from behind her.

Nancy turned around, startled. Was he following her?

"Hi, again," Nancy said. "David, I'd like you to meet George Fayne. George, this is David Carlyle."

"Oh, hello," said David, obviously impressed with George. "That's a very unusual name, especially for such a great-looking girl," he went on, not realizing he was poking George's sensitive spot.

"I was named after my father. His name was *Fayne* too." George smiled wearily, but David just laughed.

"I'm really doing a great job of making a fool of myself tonight. Sorry," he said with a shy smile.

"George is always making jokes," Nancy said. "You'll get used to her."

"Well, maybe we could start right now," said David, taking George in with appreciative eyes. "May I have this dance?"

George blushed under her terrific tan. "Sure," she said, shooting a look at Nancy.

Nancy watched as George and David swept across the dance floor to a hot Latin beat. Their eyes were locked together, and it wasn't hard to tell that they were getting very interested in each other.

Nancy scanned the floor looking for David's other friends, but she didn't see any of them.

When the song was over, George and David found Nancy near the judges' table. "That was fun," George said breathlessly. "But I'd better get back to work. See you later," she said, and smiled at David.

"See you," said Nancy.

"Later," said David, concentrating on George as she walked back to her table. "Your friend is quite a girl—really something else—"

"I know," Nancy said.

"You wouldn't happen to know if she has a boyfriend, would you?" he asked a little fearfully.

Nancy couldn't help smiling. "Not anyone serious, if that's what you mean."

"That's exactly what I mean." David sighed with relief.

"How about you?" Nancy asked. "Is one of the girls in your group your girlfriend?"

"No," David said, relaxed now. "They're just friends. Marcy—the one with red hair—goes with someone. And Gail's got a thing for Demetrios. Except he hates the world too much to even notice her."

"That's too bad," said Nancy.

"Oh, it's all his parents' fault," David said, only half joking. "He—and all of us—have been raised with so many secrets—"

"What kind of secrets?"

"Don't ask." David laughed. "Everything's a secret in our parents' world. My mother's been with the State Department for fifteen years, and I still don't know what she does. And most of our parents are traveling all the time too. Marcy's dad is somewhere in Central America, and Gail's father is in Spain. It can get kind of hard to keep track of them."

"Sounds pretty bleak," said Nancy.

"Ah, it's not that bad. Well, not for me, anyway," David replied.

Just as Nancy was about to ask what he meant, Frank Hardy came striding up to them.

"Hi, Nancy," said Frank. "You wanted to see me about some pictures?"

"Right," said Nancy. "Well, I'll see you, David."

"Sure," said David. "Maybe I'll go hang around the judges' table. . . ."

Frank took hold of Nancy's arm and led her to a quiet spot on the dance floor.

"I would have waited," Frank said softly in her ear. "But George said it was important."

"It is," Nancy whispered back while pre-

21

tending to smile. "Frank, are you and Joe working on an espionage case or something having to do with the CIA?"

"No way." Frank laughed. "We're trying to catch one of the crew members who steals from passengers in his spare time."

"Well, tonight I overheard two people talking about selling CIA information," Nancy said.

Frank's hand suddenly tightened on Nancy's arm. "Sorry," he said. "My father just lost a good friend who worked for the CIA. He was killed because someone sold him out. A lot of people think these espionage deals are just games. But they're not. Real people get hurt."

"I know," Nancy said seriously.

"Sorry for the lecture," Frank said, shaking his head and recovering. "Come on. I think Joe should hear about this too."

He steered Nancy over to a table and they sat down. He touched his right ear twice, and in a moment Joe Hardy carried over a water pitcher and glasses for the table.

"I couldn't see them," Nancy said, explaining the whole thing as Joe hovered over them, acting like a busboy. "But I think the man who wants to buy the secrets is posing as a crew member or is a crew member. He had a Spanish accent. The girl might be in that group we ran into this afternoon, Frank. I think they're all CIA kids. Maybe they're all in on it."

"Even that guy dancing with George?" Frank asked.

Nancy turned to look at the dance floor. George was wrapped in David's arms again as the band kept up its romantic beat. George looked so happy. How would Nancy feel if she had to tell her that David might be a traitor?

"I don't know if David's in on it or not. The only thing I know for sure is that the people I overheard arranged an exchange tomorrow morning at six on the Princess Deck."

"Well, that'll give Frank and me some time to mix with the crew tonight," Joe said. "A lot of them are from Latin America. And we'll be there tomorrow morning on the Princess Deck."

"Good," Nancy said. "I was hoping you'd say that."

Joe moved away quickly and started picking up empty punch glasses from around the room. He had already stood talking too long with Nancy and Frank.

"I'd better get back to work too," Frank said. He looked at Nancy's taut, somber face and said, "Smile. No one even knows we're on the case."

Just then, a piercing scream echoed through the ballroom, stopping all conversation cold.

Everyone turned to look at the entrance, where an elderly woman, her hair wild and her evening gown disheveled, had run blindly into the room, shrieking.

"Somebody! Help!" the woman cried. "I've just been attacked." And with that, she fell to the floor.

# Chapter

## Three

**T**HE BAND STOPPED PLAYING, and the Scavenger Hunt Dance came to a full stop, like a merry-go-round after someone has pulled its electrical cord.

No one moved. They all stood staring at the elderly woman who had collapsed in the middle of the ballroom floor.

Nancy and the Hardy brothers pushed their way to the center of the crowd surrounding the woman and saw that she was starting to regain control of herself.

At the same time, from the opposite direction, a tall, rugged, silver-haired man in his fifties wearing a stiff white uniform made his way quickly through the knot of people.

"Step aside, please," he repeated in a commanding yet warm voice. The crowd parted for him.

"It's Captain Helgesen," Joe told Nancy.

The ship's captain knelt beside the woman. "What seems to be the trouble, Mrs.—"

*"Miss* Lillian Hallock," said the woman, clutching at the captain's jacket. "And the trouble is I walked into my cabin tonight and was attacked by a man wearing a vampire mask."

"I'll need two crew members as escorts," Captain Helgesen said, standing up. "You two"—he pointed to Frank and Joe—"help Miss Hallock back to her cabin." The Hardys assisted the older woman to her feet.

Then the captain turned his attention to George, who was standing with David. "Ms. Fayne," said the captain, "please see if you can get this party going again."

"Yes, sir," George said. With a smile of regret George dropped David's arm and rushed to speak to the bandleader.

As soon as the band started playing, people began dancing again. Frank and Joe quietly led Miss Hallock out of the ballroom, with Captain Helgesen and Nancy following.

At the elevator Captain Helgesen turned to

26

Nancy. "I appreciate your concern, miss," he said. "We'll take care of this situation now."

"Captain Helgesen," Frank said. "This is Nancy Drew. She's a good friend of ours—"

"And a great detective too, sir," Joe added.

The captain said no more, allowing Nancy to accompany them. He was in a great hurry to get to Miss Hallock's cabin.

"Are you traveling alone, Miss Hallock?" Captain Helgesen asked as they walked down the corridor.

"Certainly not. It's not safe for a single woman to travel alone," she said with an ironic laugh. "My friend Faith Whitman is accompanying me."

When they reached Lillian Hallock's room, Captain Helgesen knocked on the door.

"You'll have to knock louder," Lillian said. "Faith is hard of hearing."

Captain Helgesen knocked loudly, and a sweet voice on the other side called, "I'm coming."

Faith Whitman opened the door in a fluffy robe. She was in her early seventies, but unlike Miss Hallock, she was small and frail, with stooped posture.

"Faith, I've brought the captain. Are you all right?" asked Miss Hallock loudly.

Faith nodded meekly. Her eyes grew wide with surprise as the three teenagers and the ship's captain walked in and began to search her cabin.

Joe examined the cabin door first, while Frank and Nancy surveyed the room. The cabin wasn't large. It was just one room with a long, mirrored dresser, two bed tables, two chairs, and two twin beds, one of which had been slept in. The other had a flannel nightgown and bathrobe folded at the foot. Everything seemed to be neatly in its place.

Frank paced the room and asked, "Miss Hallock, please tell us exactly what happened."

"I left the dance and came back here ready to go to bed," she said. "All the lights were out because Faith was already asleep. I didn't want to disturb her by turning on the overhead light, so I walked toward the dresser to get to the small vanity light—"

Miss Hallock led Frank to the mirrored dresser. "The man was standing *here,*" she said, pointing to a spot on the floor. "He grabbed me before I could reach the light."

"Did you notice anything special about him?" Frank asked.

"The vampire mask!" Miss Hallock said.

"I mean anything *else?*" Frank asked. "A limp? A distinctive aftershave, maybe, or a weird piece of jewelry? Did his digital watch beep the hour? Anything?"

"I don't know. It was dark. His mask was all I really saw before he shone a flashlight in my eyes," Lillian said. "He grabbed me and shoved me aside before he ran out. The whole episode took only ten seconds."

Frank looked down at the carpet and shook his head. If this were a garden or a park or a country house on a rainy night, there would be footprints. But there were no clues in the carpet.

"Was anything stolen?" Captain Helgesen asked.

Miss Whitman shook her head rapidly. "Oh, no, no. Nothing at all."

"Are you absolutely certain?" asked the captain.

"Oh, yes, I checked everything," she said. "Honestly, I don't know what a thief would want with *us.* We don't have much money, and certainly no jewels." Her voice was quiet and hesitant, in direct contrast to Miss Hallock's.

"Miss Whitman," Nancy asked politely, "where were *you* tonight?"

"Me? Why, I was—I was right here," the quiet older woman answered.

"You were *here* during the whole break-in?" Frank prodded her.

"Oh, yes, all evening," Miss Whitman replied. "I started reading a new mystery novel in bed. It was terribly exciting, and then, my goodness, I looked at the clock and saw it was after ten, so I turned off the light."

Nancy noticed a book with a red leather bookmark on the night table. "And you didn't hear anything unusual?" she asked.

Miss Hallock pointed to her own ear. "After Faith removes her hearing aid for the night— well, you could have held the dance in this room, and she wouldn't have heard it," she said.

Miss Whitman nodded.

"Well, the door wasn't forced," Joe said. "Our thief probably had a passkey, which means it may be someone on the crew."

"Of course it was someone on the crew," Miss Hallock said. "He was wearing one of your white uniforms. Didn't I say that? I saw it when he ran past me. He had dark hair, a white uniform, and a face like a vampire."

"We'll find him, I assure you," Captain Helgesen said to quiet the women. But as he bid them good night, he also asked a favor. "Ladies, I would appreciate it if you would not tell anyone else that Frank and Joe here know each other. They're working for me, but I want it kept secret. All right?" They nodded and Captain Helgesen thanked them.

Back in the hallway, however, he stepped out of his cool attitude. "It was bad enough having a thief on board, but now he has actually attacked a passenger," the captain said angrily. "Boys, I want this solved and fast—before the passengers begin to panic."

Joe gave the captain a reassuring salute.

"Ms. Drew, if you can do anything to help, also, I'd appreciate it," Captain Helgesen said.

Nancy began to say something but then stopped herself and just smiled. It didn't seem like the right moment to tell Captain Helgesen that he also had a couple of spies running around his ship.

"We could use a computer printout of the crew's schedule," Frank said. "To see who was on break between ten and ten-thirty."

"You'll have it in ten minutes," Captain Helgesen said.

But Helgesen was a superefficient captain, and they had it in five. The three friends took it to the ship's library, which was totally deserted during party time.

From the printout they learned that there were forty people on break at that time. The captain had narrowed the suspects down to eleven by eliminating anyone who didn't have dark hair. That was all that could be done with a pencil. Now Frank and Joe would have to check alibis in person.

"You'll still have to double-check, to make

sure someone didn't take an unscheduled break," Nancy said.

"Right." Joe nodded.

"Well, you know these guys better than I do," Nancy said. "I'm going to follow up a different angle—the vampire mask."

"We'll meet back here in an hour," Frank said.

"Midnight," Joe said. "The hour when vampires come out."

The ship's big clock was tolling midnight as Frank and Joe returned to the library. On the twelfth bong Nancy and George walked in.

"Hey, George," Joe called. "You were looking good out there on the dance floor tonight. Who's the big blond guy?"

George's face flushed a little, and Nancy could tell her friend already had a crush on David. And that could turn out to be a big problem.

"I thought George might be able to help me," Nancy said, reaching into her tote bag and pulling out a vampire mask.

"Hey, nice work, Drew," Joe said, applauding. "And you too, George. Where'd you find it?"

"It was in storage with the other costumes for the ship's masquerade dance," George answered. "Someone 'borrowed' it tonight, using a passkey."

"How do you know it was tonight?" asked Joe.

"It was out of place when we checked the costume room," George said. "It's always hung with a big black cape, but someone had put it on the scarecrow costume."

"And it was still damp inside from the guy breathing into it," Nancy added.

"Well," said Frank, "we were busy too. We did a lot of checking, and we're down to three names on the list. Rick, one of the bartenders in the casino; Julio, a steward; and Esteban, a busboy in the dining room. Everyone else on the list has an airtight alibi."

"Esteban?" Joe said. "I don't know why I didn't recognize his name before. I know him. He owes money to everyone but the captain. Which would give him a good motive for robbery. I know just where he hangs out too."

"Want to see if Miss Hallock recognizes him?" Frank asked.

"It's worth a try," Joe said. "I'll meet you at her cabin—soon. Oh, and bring the captain."

Joe took the elevator down to the lowest working level of the ship to look for Esteban Ruiz. He was right. Esteban was in one of the food lockers in the kitchen, listening to the radio and making himself a sandwich.

"Esteban—just the person I was looking for," Joe said.

"But how is it you found me?" asked Esteban. He sat down on the stool and stretched out his legs.

"The captain wants to see you right away," Joe said, taking a bite out of one half of Esteban's sandwich.

"Can he come here?" Esteban asked jokingly, grabbing his sandwich back. "First time I sat down all night."

"Sorry, but you know the captain."

"I just hope the boss didn't complain about me." Esteban quickly finished his sandwich and followed Joe up the companionway.

"Where are you taking me?" Esteban asked. "This isn't the way to the bridge."

"The captain's on the Empress level," Joe said.

The busboy looked confused, and Joe just shrugged. "I don't know what it's about," he said casually.

At Miss Hallock's cabin Joe knocked, and Captain Helgesen answered the door.

"Sir? You want to see me?" Esteban asked. He craned his neck, trying to see who else was inside the room.

"Esteban, would you come inside so we can talk to you, please?" Captain Helgesen said, stepping back.

"What's the deal?" Esteban said, crossing into the room.

Suddenly Lillian Hallock pushed past the captain to look more carefully at Esteban's face. "I know you!" she said, pointing at him with an unsteady hand. "You're the one!"

# Chapter

## Four

I KNOW YOU!" Lillian Hallock repeated. "You were fired from the Miami Tennis Club—for stealing!"

The busboy jumped back into the hall and bumped into Joe, who was about to enter the room.

"Esteban and Joe, come in and close the door," said Captain Helgesen. As always, his voice was commanding.

"Captain—I want you to know—" Lillian Hallock began hysterically.

"Now, just calm down, Miss Hallock. We'll get to the bottom of this," the captain replied soothingly.

"What's going on?" Esteban asked.

Captain Helgesen pointed to a chair for Esteban and then sat beside the older women, who were seated on the bed opposite Esteban. "Someone broke into this cabin tonight," he said, watching Esteban's face closely.

"Huh-uh. It wasn't me," said Esteban, shaking his head. "I don't care what she's been saying." He pointed right at Miss Hallock.

"Okay," Captain Helgesen said. "Then tell us where you were tonight between ten and ten-thirty?"

"Between ten and ten-thirty—let's see. I know. I was on the Princess Deck, having a smoke. And I know what you're going to say next. Did anyone see me? No. No one ever sees me unless something's been stolen."

The captain leaned forward, resting his elbows on his knees. "This isn't a joking matter, believe me," he said. "Were you issued a passkey?"

"No. I'm just a busboy. I don't go into the rooms," Esteban said.

The captain started to say something else, but Faith Whitman interrupted. "Lillian dear," she said, "are you absolutely certain that this is the young man who was fired from the club?"

"Well—" Miss Hallock said, drawing the word out.

"Oh, what's the difference?" Esteban said, jumping to his feet. "We poor people all steal, don't we?"

He slammed the palm of his hand against the wall and then whirled around to face everyone. "Okay, I did work at their tennis club last year, clearing away half-eaten plates of expensive food. And I did get fired for stealing. But I never stole anything. Never!"

"For heaven's sake. All this shouting," Miss Hallock said. "If you'd let me finish my sentence, I was about to say how sorry I was that you were fired."

"What?" Esteban asked.

"You see, the robberies continued even *after* you were fired," she said. "We knew you were innocent, but we couldn't find you. The club members wanted to apologize."

"Apologize?" Esteban said. He threw back his head again and laughed as if he hadn't heard right. "They just invent that word or something? Never heard anyone say it in English."

"Let's get back to tonight," Captain Helgesen said. "We don't want to make any mistakes."

"Captain, may I ask a question?" said Nancy. She, Frank, and George had quietly slipped into the room during the interrogation.

"Esteban, how long would it take you to get

from the Princess Deck to the room where the costumes are stored for the masquerade party?"

Esteban looked at her blankly. "How should I know?" he answered. "I don't even know where that room is. What's that got to do with anything?"

"I think that's all we need to know right now," the captain said, interrupting. "Esteban, I can't prove that you broke into this cabin, and I'm certainly not going to put you through another false accusation."

"What does that mean?" Esteban asked.

"For now," Captain Helgesen said, "it means I'm sorry we brought you here. Go back to your job, keep out of trouble, and don't tell *anyone* anything about what happened here tonight. That's an order."

Esteban left without saying a word. But he let his eyes do the talking; he glared at everyone in the room as he walked out.

"Well?" the captain asked the detectives.

"He says he was somewhere else, he doesn't have a passkey, and he says he doesn't know where the costumes are stored," Frank said.

"So he's not our man?" asked the captain.

"He could be lying, of course," said Joe. "But I don't think so. I'll continue to keep an eye on him in the dining room."

"I still don't know why everyone is fussing

so," said Miss Whitman. "Nothing was stolen."

"This is very difficult," Miss Hallock said.

"Ladies," Captain Helgesen said, "you've been very patient." He walked to the door and held it while Nancy, George, Frank, and Joe filed out. "Good night, ladies," said the captain. "I suggest that you keep your door locked when you're in here. And I hope this won't spoil your cruise."

In the hallway Captain Helgesen said to the four friends, "I'll be on the bridge and then I'm turning in." Then he turned and walked away.

"Doesn't he ever say what he's feeling?" George asked.

"His uniforms may wrinkle, but he never does," Frank said. "That's what makes him a captain."

"Our dad has known him for years," Joe said. Then he looked at his watch. "Whew. It's late. We'd better get some sleep so we can be up to meet our spies."

"Do you think we should tell the captain about this CIA thing yet?" Nancy asked.

"No, not yet," Frank said. "There's nothing he can do to help. And there's nowhere for these agents—or whatever they are—to go, except overboard. They *can't* get away. That's why I think this case is going to be a snap."

"Yeah," Joe agreed, putting his hands in his pockets. "All we have to do is show up at six this morning and grab these jerks."

"Okay," Nancy said. "Let's meet at five-thirty on the Princess Deck. That should give us enough time to prepare."

After that they said their good nights and went to their cabins.

As they got ready for bed, George told Nancy all about her dances with David—in great detail. Finally George fell asleep, a smile on her lips, but Nancy was too keyed up to sleep. She lay in bed in the dark, trying to understand what was really going on.

What would make a young girl—probably someone close to Nancy's own age—hate her country enough to betray it? Would somebody who was already well-off do something so horrible just for the money? Nancy doubted it somehow. With those troubling thoughts she finally drifted off to sleep.

The sun was just coming up when Nancy, George, and the Hardys met at five-thirty on the Princess Deck. Frank had a telephoto lens on his camera. Joe had two blueberry muffins in a bag and coffee in a thermos. Nancy had a worried look on her face.

"Hi, guys," Joe said, slipping on a pair of sunglasses. Then he did a double take at

George. She was wearing a shiny orange leotard and turquoise tights. "Hey, a little too subtle, George. You ought to wear something bright, you know? So our suspects will be sure to notice you."

"Very funny, Joe. I have to teach an aerobics class this morning," George explained with a laugh.

The four of them looked around. So far, they were the only ones on deck. But that should change at any minute.

"Let's do it," Frank said in a serious tone.

The outdoor decks at the back of the ship were tiered, like a wedding cake—the Princess Deck was the bottom tier. There were two long walkways on either side of the ship, leading to the Princess recreation area. And there were two companionways, or stairways. One was for crew only—to be used by stewards and busboys.

The other companionway was a public one, and it connected the Princess Deck to the Palace Deck right above it.

That meant there were four different ways for people to enter and leave the area that Frank, Joe, Nancy, and George were keeping under surveillance.

After a brief discussion, the four friends took up positions that made the most sense. Frank went up to the Palace level—one of the middle tiers on the cake. From there he had a good view down to the Princess Deck. As he gazed out at the sea, he saw a single gray shark fin cutting lazily through the water.

Joe stationed himself near the public stairway, hiding behind two large stacks of crates which were filled with sports equipment.

Nancy and George stood together out of sight down on the other stairway, which had a chain across it. The sign on the chain said Crew Only. Nancy and George could see up to the open sports area of the deck. They could also see Joe hiding behind the crates.

Then it was just a matter of waiting—and that didn't take long.

At five forty-five a woman in her thirties came down the public stairs. She passed Joe in his hiding place and briskly walked out onto the deck.

George poked Nancy. "It must be Pipeline," she said in a whisper. "She's right on time."

"She's early," Nancy corrected her friend.

Nancy felt her stomach tighten. Was this the woman whose voice she had heard the night before? Or was it someone else? Nancy had been expecting one of the five CIA kids. This was a new person—someone Nancy had never seen before.

The woman was tanned and blond and wore an oversize white T-shirt over gray sweat pants. Around her neck on a red cord she had a runner's watch, which she kept checking. She paced impatiently at the railing, looking out to sea for a few minutes. Then she found a deck chair and sat down.

"She's definitely waiting for someone," Nancy whispered. "We're halfway there."

Less than a minute later a man came onto the deck, rounding the corner from the other side of the ship. He was wearing the white uniform of the S.S. *Duchess*.

This was it. The rendezvous. Pipeline and the crew member Nancy had overheard!

"Who is he?" Nancy whispered to George. "Do you know him?"

"It's Pete Porter, the ship's first mate," George whispered back.

Pete Porter was a round-faced man, middle-aged, with ruddy cheeks and silver hair. He wasn't remotely Spanish-looking. Would he have a Spanish accent? He walked to the rail, smoking a pipe, and flipped a coin into the water.

Was that a signal? Nancy and George waited and watched, but the woman didn't move.

Finally Pete Porter strolled across the deck toward the young woman. He was looking right at the stairway where Nancy and George were hiding. As he passed the young woman, he tipped his hat, and she asked him for the time. Then she quickly checked her watch again. The first mate walked past her.

"What's going on?" George asked.

"He's not the right guy," Nancy whispered.

At six o'clock exactly a young man came up the portside stairway carrying a gym bag. He was in his twenties and had straight jet black hair. Nancy thought he might be from Central or South America. When he saw the woman sitting in the middle of the deck, he looked as if he wanted to turn around and leave. Instead, he slowly tied his shoe and walked to the rail. He was short, and his Bermuda shorts made him look even shorter.

"Uh-oh," George said, poking Nancy suddenly. "We've lost Frank."

Nancy looked up and saw Frank shaking hands with a strong-looking, robust man of about fifty. The man's light blue summer suit was expensive and hand-tailored, and the polished walking stick he carried was hand-carved.

"Not now, Frank," Nancy said softly to herself. "The other spy will be here any second!"

But Frank was trapped.

Up on the Palace Deck the man was introducing himself to Frank in a voice that was as firm as his handshake. "Mr. Bresson! My name is Baron Gustav von Hoffman," he said. "Most people just call me Gus."

He spoke with an accent that didn't sound exactly German but seemed to be a combination of several dialects. His manner was correct and polite.

"I've been admiring your camera since yesterday. If you wouldn't mind telling me, what film are you shooting?"

Frank swallowed. The last thing he needed was to get into a long discussion with a camera buff.

"Uh, I use different film for different situations," Frank said. He tried to sound aloof so the guy would get the message and leave him alone.

"May I see the camera?" the baron asked.

Out of the corner of his eye Frank caught a glimpse of George's bright orange leotard and wondered if anyone else might be able to see her too.

"Sorry," Frank told Baron von Hoffman. "I'm watching for whales. I have to be ready to shoot if one surfaces." He held his camera to his eye and pretended to scan the water.

Just then a handsome, muscular man bolted up the public stairs and onto the Princess Deck. He ran straight to the woman with the runner's watch. He pulled her to her feet and wrapped her in a warm embrace. They kissed for so long, they could have been mistaken for a statue.

Nancy and George were watching the marathon kiss.

"What's that?" George asked. "A new official spy greeting?"

Nancy shook her head. "I think we can forget about her. I honestly believe Pipeline is a lot younger and the people I overheard last night haven't shown up yet."

George and Nancy looked at their watches at the same time. It was 6:15 A.M.

"Hey! Look. There's someone new!" George said.

He was a lean young man with spiky black hair and an unshaven, unfriendly face. He had on an extra-large white dress shirt tucked into black jeans, and heavy black boots. Every move he made was full of arrogance. He threw himself into one of the deck chairs as if he dared it to break.

"That's one of David's friends. His name is Demetrios. His father works in the Greek embassy, and according to David, he's got a real chip on his shoulder," George said.

"Oh, no," exclaimed Nancy. "He's found Joe's hiding place."

Demetrios had bolted out of his chair and was walking straight to the area where Joe was hiding.

Demetrios pushed the storage boxes aside and glared at Joe. "What are you doing? Why are you hiding back there?"

"Me? Hiding? I was just standing here enjoying the view," said Joe.

But Demetrios wouldn't back down. He jerked Joe forward by his shirt. "I don't like people spying on me," Demetrios said. "Who are you working for?"

Joe wriggled out of Demetrios's grasp, and the two stood looking at each other as if they might explode. "Look, I don't know who you are," Joe said, "but I'll bet you were voted most likely to get bruised."

"You haven't answered my questions," Demetrios said, stepping closer to Joe.

Joe took a deep breath and then said with a cool smile, "I wasn't spying on you, so just keep your hands off me, okay?"

Joe started to walk away, but Demetrios sprang at him from behind. The force of the impact carried both of them straight toward the railing. Joe tried to stop his momentum, but the ocean was rough just then. The boat dipped in the same direction that they were moving.

Suddenly Demetrios, realizing just how

close they were to the railing, let go of Joe. Freed of the extra weight on his back, Joe lurched forward and hit the railing.

"Look out!" Frank shouted from the deck above.

But his warning came too late. Joe was tumbling headfirst over the rail—and into the shark-infested waters below!

# Chapter

## Five

"H<small>ELP</small>!"

"Man overboard!"

"Somebody help!"

The morning quiet was shattered by screams. Nancy, who had come out of her hiding place when the fight began, watched Joe fall into the water. She darted a quick glance at Demetrios standing next to her. His hands appeared to be welded to the rail, his jaw clamped tightly shut. She couldn't read his expression perfectly, but she thought he looked terrified.

George had run as fast as she could to the nearest deck telephone to call the bridge.

On the Palace Deck above, Frank shouted "No!" when Joe hit the water and disappeared under the surface.

A hand grabbed Frank's shoulder roughly. It was Baron von Hoffman. "Where are the life preservers?" the baron asked. "There must be some we can throw."

But Frank wouldn't budge from the rail—not until he saw Joe bob to the surface. Finally, after what seemed an eternity, Joe's head did appear, and Frank sprang to life.

"There's no time to lose," said the baron. "The water is very salty—it increases buoyancy. He'll float. Believe me."

But Frank was already moving. He ran to a storage bin with the word Emergency stenciled across it in big red letters. Inside there were several round white life preservers.

"Faster, faster," the baron shouted as Frank grabbed two life preservers and ran back to the railing. "His enemy is fatigue, not the water. It may take an hour for the rescue boats to reach him. We'll be miles away in minutes."

The ship slowed. Nancy and George could only stand at the rail and watch the sailors lower three long orange-painted motor launches into the water. Rescue teams scrambled into life jackets and leapt into the boats. As soon as the boats hit the water, they began motoring back to Joe.

"There he is!" George shouted, looking through borrowed binoculars and pointing.

A figure, a small dot on the water's surface, rode the waves, clutching a white life preserver. Frank sighed, relieved, when he saw Joe inside the life preserver he had tossed into the water.

"Joe's a super swimmer. He'll make it," George said.

He'll make it, Nancy thought, if he didn't break an arm or his neck in the fall. And if he doesn't run into a shark.

She and George watched silently, and so did Frank. He couldn't afford to let the whole crew know that he and Joe were brothers. It was hard not to show his feelings, but the brothers had been undercover before. They knew how to keep up a front.

Half an hour later the announcement came from the captain. "Ladies and gentlemen, the rescue operation has been successful. The young man, I'm happy to say, is unharmed. And we'll be sailing again in just a short while."

When Demetrios heard that Joe had lived through the fall, he backed away from the rail and disappeared. Nancy started to go after him but stopped. Where can he go to? she thought. I can catch him anytime. Besides, Joe's fall was an accident—wasn't it?

Or was it a diversion? Nancy wondered if she had fallen for the oldest trick in the book. Did the CIA disk transaction take place behind her back while she and everyone else were watching Joe fall into the water?

Were David and his friends really the children of CIA professionals? She didn't know for sure, but Nancy promised herself that from then on, she would treat them as if they were—and as if they were willing to sell government secrets.

"What now?" George asked when the rescue operation was over. She lowered her voice. "Do you still think there's a chance Pipeline is going to show up?"

"No, it's over for now," Nancy said. "Either it didn't go down or we blew it. I don't know which. But there's no point hanging around here any longer. I'm hungry—want to get something to eat?"

"Definitely," George said. "I've got about twenty minutes before I have to teach a class."

They walked to the dining room, and while George ate a light high-protein breakfast and Nancy nibbled at her sweet roll, they tried to figure out what had gone wrong.

"A girl with CIA secrets to sell and a man with a Spanish accent were supposed to meet this morning," Nancy said. She leaned forward so that George could hear her in the loud, crowded dining room. "But did they meet? We really don't know what happened. Now, what's the worst scenario?"

"We were in the wrong place, and they met somewhere else," George said.

Nancy nodded. "But I *heard* them make the appointment. They agreed to meet on the Princess Deck at six."

"But obviously they didn't show," said George. "Could they have overslept? Or been seasick?"

"It's too much of a coincidence that they *both* didn't show," Nancy said. "I think the buyer was there. He sounded like a pro, as if he knew what he was doing."

"You mean we actually *saw* him?" George said. "Well, who do you think it was? The first mate? The guy in the Bermuda shorts? The Romeo, who went for the world's record on kissing?"

"There were a lot of guys—but no girls. At least not the right one," Nancy said. Then she noticed that George's attention had drifted away. Nancy followed her friend's gaze— David Carlyle had just walked into the dining room with three of his friends. With David were Demetrios, the blond girl, Gail, and another boy, Connor, the one who wore tortoise-shell glasses. The group sat down somberly, staring at the tablecloth as the waiter filled their cups with steaming coffee.

George's brown eyes were fixed on their table. "He doesn't see me," she said, smiling softly.

"George—" Nancy began. "I know how much you're attracted to David, and I think that's great, but I really hope you're being careful—"

George picked up a piece of whole-wheat bread and looked steadily at Nancy. "What are you trying to tell me?"

"Well, David and those other kids—there's a good chance they're CIA kids. And there's a possibility they could get hold of some pretty heavy government secrets to sell if they wanted to."

George's eyes widened. "Wait just a minute. You're not saying that you think David's involved in all this spy business, are you?"

"I'm not sure," said Nancy. "Anything is possible. And I'd hate for you to get hurt. It makes sense to me that it was Gail or Marcy I heard on the steps last night. And then I have to ask myself what was David doing there at the same time? And why was Demetrios on the Princess Deck this morning just when a disk was to be sold? Was he supposed to create a diversion so no one would see the computer disk being exchanged? And why isn't Marcy sitting with them right now? You see? I've got a lot of questions, George."

George slumped back in her chair. "Why is this happening?" she moaned. "I meet a guy who makes bells ring for me, and my best friend thinks he may be a traitor! This is driving me crazy. Come on, Nancy. I have a class to teach, thank goodness. Feel like working out? I know *I* do!"

Nancy sighed with relief. George sounded like herself again. "Sure. Let's go for the burn."

Meanwhile Frank Hardy was in Joe's cabin, watching his brother get into his busboy uniform.

"You've got enough tape around you to be a Christmas package," Frank said with a whistle.

"Everyone should start his day off with a swim in the sea and a couple of bruised ribs. I recommend it," Joe said. He was moving stiffly, but his sense of humor was in good shape. "Did you find out which cabin Demetrios is in? He and I have to finish our 'conversation.'"

"If you really want to know, you can look it up. He's on the passenger list," Frank said. "But I think you ought to cool out for a while first. Besides, we have a lot to do today. Remember why we're here. We have to nab a thief. The captain's counting on us, and he expects results."

"Yeah, you're right. First things first," Joe said. "So how's it going with our plan and our imaginary buddy, the millionaire? Do you think the crew will believe Maxwell Schweidt is real?"

"While you were getting your ribs taped, I started to set the trap," Frank explained. "I put some clothes in an empty stateroom, E two seventeen, and I hooked up a silent alarm on the door." He showed Joe a small electronic beeper in his pocket. "This will go off if anyone opens the door—even if a passkey is used. I also entered Maxwell Schweidt's name on the passenger list and put him at the captain's table in the dining room. And this afternoon I've scheduled an appointment to take his photograph."

"Great," Joe said, taking a crisp fifty-dollar bill out of his wallet and putting it in his white jacket pocket.

"What's that for?" Frank asked.

"Maxwell Schweidt's a big tipper, didn't you know?" Joe said with a wink. "I'm going to tell the crew I got this for bringing him a newspaper and a couple of magazines. Sounds like pretty good bait, doesn't it?"

"Let's hope our cabin thief thinks that Maxwell Schweidt is a target he can't resist. Then when he breaks into Maxwell's room and the alarm goes off, we'll be there to grab him. Is this all sneaky enough for you, younger brother?"

"Frank," Joe said, smiling, "it's great to see that I'm finally having an influence on you!"

"According to rumor, you know," said Frank, "Schweidt made his fortune in a South African diamond mine—"

"Right!" replied Joe. "That explains all those diamond rings the guy has—"

"And why he always carries money in several different currencies."

"Well, when you own banks, you do that."

Frank Hardy had his hand on the door. "Very convincing, Joe. I believed you, and I *know* Maxwell Schweidt doesn't exist!"

"Come on! Stretch it out—one and two and three and four!"

The music in the health club was pounding, and George had to shout to be heard. She was leading a group of about two dozen passengers in a grueling aerobics routine.

Nancy stood at the back of the class, bouncing in time to the music, hoping the exercise would help to clear her head.

It was more than two hours since the fiasco

on the Princess Deck, and still she had only questions. Who? Why? Where? What, she knew—CIA secrets. Codes, maps, plans, the girl had said. Real people get hurt, Frank Hardy had said. But where were the answers?

Just then the mirrored door to the health spa opened, and David Carlyle walked in. He was with his friend Gail. What a break, Nancy thought. This would be the perfect time to try to hear Gail's voice. But if Gail were Pipeline, would Nancy recognize her voice after so much time?

Nancy watched George in the front of the room move in time with the music, but she noticed George's eyes were fixed on David. She gave him a smile, but David seemed to ignore her. His face looked tight with worry. He and Gail were scanning the room as if they were searching for someone. Finally George appeared as if she couldn't take it anymore.

She stopped the routine, and with her hands on her hips, she called to them loudly, "Can I help you?"

David looked up and seemed to notice George for the first time. "George!" he said, surprised.

"Come on, David," Gail insisted, yanking him by the arm. "Let's get out of here!"

David looked as if he wanted to say more to George, a lot more, but finally he shook his head in frustration and followed Gail out the door.

Nancy fell out of the line and rushed through the swinging doors. "David!" Nancy called, catching up with him and Gail in the hallway. "Is something wrong?"

"Uh, I hope not. We were just looking for someone. Marcy, that is," David said, his voice sounding strained. "But she wasn't there. That's all."

Nancy looked at Gail. The blond girl shot her a bored look and tossed her hair. But Nancy could tell that she was trying to hide her feelings. Her eyes had a kind of panic in them.

"Can I help?" Nancy offered.

"No!" said Gail, a little more fiercely than she intended to, thought Nancy. "I mean, it's okay—"

"Did you guys argue or something?" Nancy suggested. "Maybe she just wanted to be alone for a while. Or maybe she met someone—"

"Oh, stop it!" Gail blurted out. "You don't know anything about us!"

"Oh?" asked Nancy. "Like what?"

Angry tears welled up in Gail's eyes. "We stick together—and we *don't* need you or anyone else!" With that, Gail broke down, sobbing.

"David," Nancy said, "let me help you. You can hide, but you can't disappear on a ship. I know some of the staff—they may know hiding places—"

"The trouble is, Nancy, we've looked everywhere. Everywhere. Marcy's gone. Vanished." David was completely pale.

"It's worse than that! Something horrible has happened to her," cried Gail with absolute finality. "I know it! Marcy's *dead!*"

# Chapter

## Six

"Marcy's dead?" Nancy asked. "How do you know?"

Gail shook her head and rubbed her hands across her face. "I don't *know*—it's just a feeling," she murmured. "Just forget it, okay?"

"Forget it?" Nancy asked incredulously. "How can I do that?" But Gail had shut herself off from Nancy, and she turned to David with an icy stare. "Come on, let's go," she said, tugging on his arm.

David shot a look of distress to Nancy, but he went along with Gail. "I guess we'll keep looking, Nancy—"

"David! Come on!" Gail insisted, irritated

now. That voice was definitely *not* the voice Nancy had heard on the steps that day. And if Gail wasn't Pipeline, Nancy was almost positive that Marcy *was*.

"I'll have the captain make an announcement, David," Nancy called after them. "Don't worry, we'll find her."

Unless she's fallen overboard, of course, thought Nancy with a shudder. Or unless she was pushed . . .

To Nancy's surprise, she found the captain in his office when she knocked on his door at noon.

"Come in, Ms. Drew," Captain Helgesen said from behind his desk. His office was filled with computers and navigation equipment as well as antique nautical compasses. "Any news about our cabin thief?"

"No," said Nancy, taking the chair opposite him. "Captain Helgesen," she began, her bright blue eyes meeting his steely gray ones. "I hate to tell you this, but something very dangerous is happening on the *Duchess*—something potentially more dangerous than theft."

The captain listened glumly as Nancy filled him in on everything that had happened so far, from the conversation on the stairway to Marcy's disappearance.

"Her friends have searched all the public areas. She's nowhere to be found," Nancy ended.

"And this was the same girl you heard on the steps?" the captain asked, concerned.

"I don't know that for sure," Nancy said. "But there are very few young people on board. And the voice was definitely young. I think she could have been the one. And if I'm right, there's a good reason to suspect she may be a victim. Is there any chance of making a room-by-room sweep?"

"That would be all my passengers need," the captain muttered. "Between Miss Hallock and her attacker and Joe Hardy falling overboard—" But as he spoke he was furiously scribbling something on a small piece of paper.

Then he hit the intercom button on his telephone. A first mate appeared instantly. "Make this announcement over the P.A. system every half hour," the captain said.

"Aye, aye, sir. 'Will Marcy Durbanville please come to the captain's bridge,'" he read.

"That's right," the captain nodded. "If she's anywhere on the ship, this should get her attention."

It should have, but it didn't. For a while Nancy waited in the captain's office, hoping Marcy would show up. Finally she couldn't sit still any longer. She left and, one by one, found Frank, Joe, and George, and filled them in on Marcy's disappearance. Then she checked around all the dark and deserted places on the ship—hoping to find someone who wanted to get lost. But there was no Marcy.

The fourth time she heard the message on the loudspeakers, Nancy went back to the bridge. It had been more than two hours, and no Marcy.

"All right, all right. We'll make that sweep," said the captain before Nancy could say a word. "I'll send two of my crew to work with you. There are six hundred and thirty-two cabins on the *Duchess*. It's going to take hours to search them all."

Nancy's solution to that was to break the search into two teams. Frank Hardy and a second mate took the two upper decks, and Nancy, along with a purser named Elliot, took the lower ones. It was like another scavenger hunt, except there was only one item on the list: Marcy Durbanville.

The search was slow, monotonous, and difficult. Following the captain's orders, they knocked at each door twice and waited half a minute or more before using the passkey to enter.

As Nancy and Elliot approached Marcy and

Gail's cabin, Nancy hoped they'd find it empty. It would be a perfect opportunity to take a look.

The purser knocked on the door. He had lost his smile twenty cabins earlier. For a couple of minutes there was no answer.

Then the door opened a crack.

"What's going on?" Gail asked, frowning.

Nancy peeked around Elliot. "Gail, we're searching every room for Marcy," she said.

Gail didn't open the door any wider. "Well, she's not in here," said Gail with a sarcastic laugh.

"Can I come in?" asked Nancy.

"No, not now," Gail answered, shutting the door rudely.

Elliot went right on to the next cabin door, which was David and Connor's. He knocked. No one answered.

Great, Nancy thought. At least I'll get to look around in there.

But when Elliot opened it with the passkey, someone pushed the door closed again from the inside. "Nobody home," a voice called. It wasn't David's voice, so it must have been Connor's.

"Real friendly group of passengers," Elliot said, shaking his head.

* * *

Meanwhile Frank and his partner, a sailor who was called Slow Motion Moe by most of the crew, were searching cabins on the two upper decks.

Frank looked at the passenger list on his clipboard and sighed. The next cabin belonged to Baron and Baroness von Hoffman. Ever since that morning on the Palace Deck, the baron had been hounding Frank to talk to him about photography. "Moe, you've got to do me a favor."

"Oh, yeah?" Moe challenged in his deep voice.

"Let me say it another way," Frank said. "Moe, would you do me a favor?"

"Why?" Moe said.

"I'll tell you what the favor is. I want you to check this cabin without me. I can't handle a long conversation with the guy in there. Okay? No big deal?"

"No big deal," Moe said. "But what did you come along for?"

Frank didn't answer. He just stood off to the side, out of sight, as Moe knocked on the baron's door.

"Good afternoon," said the baron, opening the door. "What may I do for you?"

"Got to inspect your cabin. Plumbing."

"I've seen no leaks," said the baron.

"Got to inspect your cabin. Plumbing."

"Well, I guess I only have to be told twice," said the baron with a chuckle. "Do come in. However, would you be especially quiet? My wife is not feeling well, and she's napping on the bed."

"Don't have to inspect the bed. Plumbing," Moe said, stepping into the baron's cabin. "Hey—it smells funny in here."

The cabin door closed. A few moments later the door opened and Moe rejoined Frank in the hall. And then, to Frank's dismay, so did the baron! He and Frank stared at each other for a moment.

"Frank!" said the surprised baron. "How fortunate running into you. You'll never guess what I'm going to ask you. It's a very simple question. I want to photograph the sunset with a fifty-millimeter lens. What f-stop should I use, and am I better off using a fast film or a slow one?"

The very simple question turned into a very lengthy discussion, and since Frank was crew, he had to stand tough and take it. After about ten minutes Frank was ready to tell the baron to buy an instant camera and stop worrying.

Finally, when the baron excused himself to check on his wife, Frank moved down the hall—and ran right into Joe.

"Moe," Frank said, "I'll catch up with you

in a minute." Frank waited until Moe was inside the next cabin and then turned to his brother. "What's up?"

Joe put a piece of gold jewelry in Frank's hand.

It was a large gold cuff link, with lots of diamonds and very expensive.

"Look what I found," Joe said. "It was sort of hidden under a stack of life preservers on the Empress Deck."

"So? I don't get why you're showing it to me," Frank said.

"Listen," said Joe, "I've done some checking. No one's reported it missing or stolen. And, believe me, if I lost this little gold mine, I'd be checking the lost-and-found every ten minutes. Wouldn't you?"

"Yes, so?"

"So," Joe went on, "maybe the person who lost this doesn't want it to be found."

"Why not?" Frank said.

"Who knows? Maybe it has bloodstains on it. Or maybe it has fingerprints. Too bad we don't have a forensics lab on board."

"Yeah," Frank said. "But I won't believe there's anything fishy until we try to find its owner."

"Okay," Joe said. "I'll get George to make an announcement at dinner. Meanwhile, keep your ears open."

After he was down the hall a few steps, Joe asked confidentially, "How's the search going?"

"Nothing yet," Frank answered.

"Maybe you'll catch the cabin thief while you're looking for Marcy."

"Fat chance," Frank said glumly.

"How's Nancy doing?"

"I wish I knew," Frank said.

Nancy and the purser had already inspected more than fifty rooms. "Well, only a few hundred more to go," the purser said, joking.

Nancy managed a wan smile.

"You don't talk much, do you, Nancy?" asked Elliot as they walked up to the next door.

"Sorry, Elliot," Nancy said. It was hard to be friendly when she knew there might be a corpse in the next closet she opened.

"What are we doing?" Elliot asked, laughing. "This is your cabin." Sure enough, they were standing in front of Cabin Thirty-seven.

"Well, she's not in there, but you should check it, I suppose. I'll go around the next corridor and start there."

"Meet you in a couple of minutes," said Elliot.

Rounding the corner, Nancy started down another long hallway. These rooms were mostly staff quarters. She knocked on the first door. No answer. She knocked again. Still no answer. Reaching for the passkey the captain had given her, she opened the door.

It was dark and quiet inside. As Nancy reached for the light switch, a man's thick, hairy arm grabbed her from behind. It came around her throat and pulled her chin up so she couldn't breathe. Like a vise, his hand held her shoulders tight.

Before Nancy could yell, before she could even think, she felt a cold sharp edge at her throat. She didn't need the lights to know what it was. It was a knife!

# Chapter

## Seven

**W**HAT DO YOU WANT?" the man holding
Nancy asked in a deep, raspy voice.

The arm around Nancy's throat gripped
even tighter. She didn't dare move with the
knife so close to her throat. So she froze,
hoping her silence would make her attacker
relax.

It worked.

He backed away a little and kicked the cabin
door closed before snapping on the light.

Nancy turned around slowly to face a small
man in a white uniform and a tall chef's hat.
Around his waist was a black leather holster

for a long kitchen knife. But the knife wasn't in its holster. It was pointed at Nancy.

"What are you doing in my cabin?" he asked.

"I'm part of a plumbing-inspection team," Nancy said.

The man jerked the knife toward Nancy as a warning. "You're not a plumber, and you're not crew," he snarled. "So what are you doing in my room?"

There was a knock on the door. Nancy didn't move or utter a sound.

Another knock. "Nancy, are you in there?" Elliot said from the hallway.

Nancy looked at the cook before answering, "Yes!"

The cook tapped the knife flat against the back of his hand. "Nobody comes in my cabin again. Now get out."

Nancy opened the door quickly and ran out.

"Find anything?" Elliot asked.

"A very strange guy. He had a knife like this," Nancy said, holding her index fingers about ten inches apart.

"Oh, I'm sorry. Really sorry. I shouldn't have left you alone." Elliot winced. "I thought Chef Borka would be in the galley. He really guards his privacy."

"Why? Does he have anything to hide?" Nancy asked.

"No one's ever dared to ask," said Elliot.

When they were almost done, Frank and Slow Motion Moe caught up with them. At Nancy's questioning look Frank shook his head. They hadn't found Marcy either.

After that they finished their search without anything dramatic happening.

"So what are the possible explanations?" the captain asked when Nancy reported that they hadn't found Marcy.

"One: she fell overboard. Two: she was murdered and thrown in the ocean. Three: she was kidnapped and hidden somewhere on the ship." Nancy laid the possibilities out for the captain methodically because she knew that was what he wanted.

"Well, it's my ship. I'm going to assume she's gone overboard," Captain Helgesen said. "Until you prove otherwise. Now I'll call in her friends to inform them."

"Captain," Nancy broke in, "would you mind very much if *I* told them? It might help me find out a few things."

The captain considered for a moment. "I don't see any reason why not," he said.

"Thanks." Nancy was pleased. Breaking the news to Marcy's friends might be very useful. But first she had to organize her thoughts. She went down to the promenade on the Palace level and sat down in a deck chair. Piano music drifted out of the Paradise Lounge during the predinner hour.

It was strange to watch passengers walk by, laughing and having a good time, while she and the Hardys were dealing with something so evil.

Nancy looked up and saw a man at the far end of the promenade. He seemed to be staring at her. That's odd, Nancy thought to herself. She didn't recognize him. Why was he watching her?

A moment later the man walked away, and Nancy relaxed. Maybe it was nothing. In any event, it was time to pay a visit to Gail to let her know that the search for Marcy had been a washout.

Nancy knocked on the cabin door that Gail and Marcy shared. "Just stay calm," she said, steeling herself. It wasn't going to be easy.

But Nancy was in for a shock. When Gail answered the door, she was actually smiling! "Oh, it's you," she said perkily.

"Gail, I'm sorry," Nancy said. "We didn't find her."

"Oh?" Gail said flatly. "Well, it's okay. She'll turn up, I guess." With that, she started to close the door.

"Wait a minute," said Nancy, holding it open. "What's going on here?"

"Who is it, Gail?" asked a voice inside the room.

Gail looked at Nancy and looked behind her as if she couldn't make up her mind about something. Finally she moved away from the door so Nancy could come in. "Nothing's going on here," she said, her smile vanishing. "See for yourself."

Demetrios, David, and Connor were all sitting on the couch watching television with the volume turned way up, but Nancy knew she hadn't heard the television when Gail came to the door.

What was happening? Nancy wondered. None of Marcy's friends seemed to care that she had disappeared. But why? Was it an act they were putting on for Nancy's benefit? Or had something changed—something basic—since that morning, when Gail was so upset?

"Can I look around at Marcy's stuff?" Nancy asked.

"What?" asked Gail. She couldn't hear Nancy because Demetrios kept turning up the sound with the remote control.

Nancy tried again, but Demetrios had his thumb on the remote control volume. The three guys didn't look at her. They just stared at the television.

"Turn it down," Gail finally shouted, and Demetrios lowered the volume a little.

"I don't want to break up the fun," Nancy said, "but I was just all over this ship looking for Marcy, and I didn't find her."

"So much for the great detective." Demetrios snickered.

It was a contagious snicker—everyone caught it except Nancy.

"Don't you care if she's in trouble?" Nancy asked, looking directly at David. He seemed very uncomfortable, even embarrassed. But he didn't come to her rescue.

"Who doesn't care? Of course we care," he said defensively. "We're her friends."

"You could have fooled me," Nancy replied. Was this the same guy George was falling so hard for? It was as if David were a different person when he was with his friends.

"We're not trying to fool you," Demetrios explained, the cruel snicker resurfacing in his voice. "We're trying to ignore you. What's happened to Marcy is none of your business."

"No, it's not my business that a passenger is missing. It's the captain's business. And he's very concerned. In fact, he's about to notify her parents."

Demetrios laughed.

"Fine. Let him try," Connor said. "Her father's on assignment in Central America somewhere, and her mother's been dead for years."

"David—what about you? Is this all *you're* going to do? Sit here and pretend nothing's going on?" Nancy asked.

"Look, Nancy. We'll take care of it, okay?" David said more gently this time. "I'm sorry I got you involved."

"Yeah—bye," Connor said, picking up the remote control and turning the volume up.

Nancy stared at the four blank faces. There was no sense in trying to get through to them. Without another word she walked out of the room. A couple of steps down the hall and she heard the door slam behind her.

She went straight to the dining room. Dinner was being served, and Nancy was hungry. But more important, she had to talk to George. Nancy had to warn her about David before the budding romance went any further. It wasn't that Nancy didn't like David—she did—but he was hiding something, she just knew it, something dangerous.

"Hi, Nancy! Wish I had time to sit with you, but we're getting everything ready for the lotto game tonight." George was gone before Nancy could say a thing to her.

Sitting down at a table, Nancy decided to eat before she even considered what her next steps would be.

She was just finishing her meal, when someone tapped her shoulder. David Carlyle was standing beside her.

"Is this seat taken?" he asked shyly, indicating the empty chair next to Nancy. When she shook her head no, he sat down and smiled at her as if nothing had happened.

"George really looks great tonight, doesn't she?" he remarked, nodding toward where George was standing, wearing a teal blue jumpsuit.

"She always looks great," Nancy said pointedly, trying to figure David out.

"Nancy, maybe you could give me a little advice," he stammered, blushing a bit. "What's the best way to impress her? I mean, you've known her for a long time, and—"

"David," Nancy said, interrupting him, "is that why you sat down here? To ask me how to impress George? You seem to be forgetting what just happened down in your cabin."

David looked down at the table. "Oh. That," he said. "I'm sorry I acted so weird—" He started playing with a napkin as he spoke.

"David, something happened between this morning and now—something having to do with Marcy. Everything's changed, hasn't it?"

David nodded slowly, silently.

"Have you found Marcy?" Nancy asked him. "Have you heard from her?"

"No," David said. "But we're pretty sure we know what's going on. So don't worry about it anymore. Really."

Nancy turned to face him. Did David really want her to let it go at that? "Okay, what's going on?" she asked.

"We decided not to talk about it," David said.

"I see," Nancy said. "And did everyone decide you should apologize?"

"No," David said, raking his fingers through his hair. "That was my idea. I acted like a jerk, and I know it. Can you forgive me?"

Nancy relaxed a little. "All right," she finally said. "Apology accepted. But, David, I wonder if you realize what you're getting into—the people you're dealing with are dangerous. I can help, but you've got to trust me."

David studied her, biting his lip. He seemed unsure.

"Attention, everyone!" George was standing on the dais, microphone in hand. "I have a couple of announcements to make. First of all, a man's valuable cuff link has been found. If you've lost it, please contact me. And if you don't want it back, please lose the other one so I'll have a matched pair.

"After dinner tonight," George continued, "the movie in the theater is *Singin' in the Rain,* and the dance in the disco is a fifties sock hop. So come dressed to jitterbug!" George turned off her microphone and started for Nancy's table.

"Hi," David said, standing up when George got there. "Nancy and I were just talking about you."

"Oh, good," George said, smiling as she sat down. "Don't let me stop you. Just pretend I'm not here."

David took out a piece of folded ship's stationery from his pocket and said, "I have a short list of questions I'd like to ask you about your friend George, Nancy."

Nancy put on a very serious face and nodded that she was ready.

"What is George's favorite perfume? Isn't she afraid of anything? What's—"

But before David could say anything more, Joe Hardy interrupted them. He appeared out of nowhere and started pouring ice water into Nancy's glass. "I've got news," he whispered in her ear. "Meet me in E two seventeen in fifteen minutes." Then he walked away.

Nancy glanced over to see if David had noticed anything, but he was gazing at George. The two of them looked as if they'd forgotten Nancy's presence completely. Guess it won't be too hard to get away, Nancy thought. They won't even notice I'm gone.

"Well, I'm off," Nancy announced a few

minutes later. "I want to get to the library before it closes."

"Bye, Nancy. See you later," said George. George probably thought Nancy was just giving her a chance to be alone with David.

When Nancy got to cabin E two seventeen, Joe Hardy was waiting.

"Whose cabin is this?" Nancy asked as he closed the door behind her.

"Maxwell Schweidt's," Joe said. "He won't mind if we use it—believe me, he won't mind. He's a passenger Frank and I invented to trap the cabin thief."

"Nice idea," Nancy said. "But that's not what you wanted to tell me."

"Huh-uh," Joe said with a devilish look on his face. "It's better than *tell*. I have something to *show* you."

Nancy laughed and braced herself for what might be a practical joke. "Okay, what is it?" she asked with her hands on her hips.

"This." Joe held up a piece of white paper. "I found this note on the bulletin board in the crew locker room," he said triumphantly.

"You *took* it?" Nancy asked.

"Of course not. I copied it down," Joe said. "I left the original there."

"What does it say?"

Joe read from the slip of paper.

"For sale: *Very* valuable collection of compact disks still available. Will exchange for information about *Pipeline*. Leave message in cabin A forty-three."

"Pipeline!" Nancy said. "That's the girl's code name. And the rest of that note is in code too, I'll bet. Compact disks must mean computer disks."

"Right," Joe said. "But you aren't asking the numero uno question."

"Oh? What's that?" Nancy asked.

Joe held up the piece of paper and snapped it with his finger.

"Who wrote the note?"

# Chapter

## Eight

"WHO WROTE THE NOTE?" Nancy said, repeating Joe's words. "Who sleeps in Cabin A forty-three?"

"No one," said Joe with a wry grin. "It's unoccupied. So the question remains—who wrote the note?"

"It makes no sense. It sounds like the note should have been written by Pipeline, since she was selling the information. But why does she ask for information about herself?" Nancy said, seating herself on a chair.

Just then the cabin door flew open. Nancy and Joe jerked their heads toward the intruder and jumped up.

"Sorry I'm late," Frank Hardy said, hurrying in. "What's up?"

"Joe has some big news," Nancy told him. She sat down again.

"I found the original of this on the bulletin board in the crew's locker lounge," Joe explained, handing his brother the paper.

Frank read the note and sat down on Maxwell Schweidt's bed. "Whoa," Frank said. "This is getting more complicated all the time."

"Here he goes," Joe said with a smile. "He's going to start asking himself a million questions now."

"Typical private investigator's kid," Nancy said teasingly. "But seriously, what would happen if we started at the beginning and looked at everything methodically?"

"Typical lawyer's kid," Frank said, a slow grin lighting up his face.

Nancy returned the grin, then they began in earnest. "Okay," Joe said as he leaned against the dresser. "Where are we?"

"I think I've just figured it all out," Nancy said. She pulled her chair closer to the Hardys. "According to the note, the disks are *still* for sale, which means we didn't blow it this morning. The exchange never took place."

"I'll go along with that," Frank said. "But why not?"

"That I don't know," Nancy replied. "Let's put that one on hold for now. The other thing the note tells us is that Pipeline has an accomplice or friend—and the accomplice doesn't know where she is. It's the only way the note makes sense."

"It's amazing. Whoever wrote this note isn't even looking for money," Joe said, flicking the paper. "He just wants to get Pipeline back!"

"I agree," Nancy said. "And since I'm convinced that Marcy is Pipeline, it makes sense that one of her friends wrote the note."

"Sounds good," Frank agreed. "The only thing I don't get is how did her friends know to put the note on the crew bulletin board?"

"Maybe," Nancy said, "Marcy met with her friends, or friend, after she met the Spanish guy on the stairs. She told them what happened. You know, it seems like they tell one another everything. So maybe it happened like this: Marcy waited on the stairs with that Plummer's bag as a signal, so the guy would know who she was. When he did show up, she saw that he was a crew member."

"But why was she meeting with someone she didn't even know?" Joe asked.

"I don't know yet," Nancy admitted. "Just follow me for a minute. After she talks to the guy on the stairs, she goes back to her friends and tells them that the contact is a busboy, or whatever. Then sometime between nine last night and five-thirty this morning, Marcy disappears. Her friends think that the contact, the crew member, had something to do with her vanishing act, but they don't know who he is. So they put up the note in the crew's lounge and hope he'll respond."

"These guys are really playing with blindfolds on," Joe said, whistling.

"Interesting," Frank said. "I guess we'll have to assume that all of her friends are in on it. As you said, they do seem to stick together."

"I don't know," Nancy said tentatively. The thought of David Carlyle being involved in all of it was disturbing. And yet, what Frank said made sense.

"Let's check out that cabin," Nancy suggested. "Frank, you leave first. Then Joe. I'll meet you as soon as the corridor is clear."

Ten minutes later they were inside Cabin A forty-three—the cabin mentioned in the bulletin-board note.

"If no one's staying here," Joe said, "I wonder why the note said to leave a message in this cabin?"

"They're using it as a drop," Frank answered. "Because it's empty, it's perfect."

"There's the message," said Nancy, pointing

to a small white paper on the bureau. She walked over, picked up the note, and read it out loud.

"I'm still interested in your disk collection. Meet me at the ruins in Cozumel. High noon, Monday. Alone. *I'll find you.*"

"I guess it pays to advertise," Frank said with an ironic smile.

"Great. Now all we have to do is sit here and wait for someone to open that door," Joe said. "And—zap—we've got whoever is selling those disks."

"No, no, no," Nancy and Frank said in unison. They turned to look at each other.

"We—" They began again at the same time.

"Ladies first," said Frank.

"Frank Hardy, I never suspected you were a chauvinist," Nancy quipped.

"All right, I give. Redheads first—is that better?"

"Uh-huh. Now, Joe, what we were going to say is, even if we grab the seller, we still have to find the buyer. That's who probably has Marcy," said Nancy.

"Okay, then, let's leave the message and get out of here," Frank said. "We don't want to mess up anything."

Joe peeked out into the hall to see if it was clear. He motioned to the others to follow him.

"So tomorrow it's the ruins at Cozumel," Nancy said as they walked past a line of stateroom doors. "We've got to be there at noon."

"That's a problem, Nancy," Frank said, shaking his head. "Joe and I are pretty sure the cabin thief will hit tomorrow while people are on shore. It's prime time, when the boat is so empty. We've got to be here to catch the thief."

"Both of us?" Joe asked.

"Good point," Frank said. "If the thief finally does hit Maxwell Schweidt's cabin, I could handle it myself."

"Great," Joe said. "Then I'll go with Nancy."

"I'll be glad to have the company," Nancy said, giving Joe a grateful smile.

"Well, I'm going to turn in," Joe said with a yawn. "I'm tired. Unlike you guys, I'm *working* on this boat. I got up at five this morning. See you at breakfast."

They watched Joe walk off. Then Frank and Nancy strolled in silence past the closed shops. Neither felt it was necessary to say a word. They ambled slowly, comfortable and close.

"Hey—I have an idea," Frank said. "How about a swim? It'll help us to relax for tomorrow."

"All the pools are closed," Nancy said. Then she turned and looked up into Frank's eyes and gave him a dazzling grin. "But who cares?"

"Best time to avoid the crowds," Frank said lazily. "Well? What do you say? Meet me at the pool on the Palace Deck in fifteen minutes."

"I'll be there!"

On the way back to her stateroom to change, Nancy thought about Frank. Was she attracted to him? she asked herself. She honestly had to answer yes. He was warm and funny and caring and, best of all, intelligent. He was almost the most special boy she knew—almost. But there was Ned, and Nancy knew Frank could only be her friend. She would have to leave it at that—and she hoped she could.

Joe Hardy stopped on the way back to his room to lean against the rail on the Princess Deck and look out to sea. He was standing in almost the same spot he had been when he went overboard. He looked down at the long drop into the water and then up at the sky.

"Hey, moon," Joe said. "You missed it. I made a great dive the other day. Dynamite form—slipped into the water like a hand into a glove."

Suddenly Joe looked around. He could

swear he heard someone crying. He was right. Just twenty feet away Gail was standing at the railing too, sobbing her heart out.

Joe watched her for a moment. The blond girl looked so small and lonely. Maybe he could help, he thought.

"Hi," he said softly, making his way toward her. "It can't be that bad—"

"Oh, it is!" Gail sobbed. "My whole life is such a mess—"

For the first time, Joe noticed that Gail was pretty. Her green eyes were so vulnerable as she looked up at him.

"I'm sorry," she murmured, glancing away. "I must be bothering you—"

"That's okay," said Joe, standing next to her. Her defenses were down, and with the hard edge gone, Gail seemed lost and frightened and very young.

"Maybe I should just give up—" She was sobbing again. "Maybe nothing is worth it all—"

Joe knew what she was thinking by the way she was looking at the water. "Hey, wait a minute. Whatever your problem is, it can't be that bad," he said.

"Oh, it is—"

"My name is Joe, by the way."

"I know. You're a busboy, right?"

"On this cruise I am," he answered, smiling at her. "But do you know what's under this white jacket?"

"A heart of gold?"

"Well, no . . . actually, it's my Sea World T-shirt."

Gail laughed in spite of herself. Then she smiled at Joe and wiped at her tears with the back of her hand. She was looking at him in a way that sent a shiver up his spine. "You seem so together," she said.

"That's me," Joe agreed with a laugh. "Problems? What are they?"

Then they looked at each other for a long moment as the boat swayed beneath them. He could see the moon reflected in her eyes.

"So, what *is* your problem?" he asked disarmingly.

Gail looked out at the sea and sighed out loud. "I really can't talk about it," she said softly.

Joe decided not to push it. "Where are your friends?" he asked her. "I thought you and your friends always breathed the same air."

"I wanted to be alone," Gail said.

"Do you still?" Joe asked quietly.

"I don't know."

"You look awfully sad," he told her.

Suddenly Gail shivered. Joe took off his jacket and slipped it over her shoulders.

"Hey," he whispered. "We don't have to talk about it. There are a million other things to talk about. That's what's nice about meeting someone new—there are endless possibilities."

Gail stood gazing into Joe's eyes, which were only inches away. Then her eyelids started to close, and she leaned in even closer.

Suddenly she was wrapped up in his arms, and their lips were pressed together. Joe's heart was pounding. He hadn't meant to kiss her, it had just happened.

When it was over, there was nothing to say. Gail leaned against him and turned her head toward the water. "That was nice," she whispered.

"*Very* nice," Joe said huskily. And he meant it.

Nancy looked at herself in the mirror in her cabin. Her new bathing suit was great. It was a tank style, cut high at the thighs and low in the back. The iridescent blue of the fabric almost perfectly matched her eyes. She threw on jeans and a sweatshirt, grabbed a towel, and stepped out of her cabin.

There was a vaguely familiar-looking man standing and observing her from the other end of the hallway. Nancy returned his stare for a moment, and then he turned and walked away.

Now, where have I seen him before, Nancy wondered. And then it came to her. He was the same man who had been staring at her that afternoon. She wondered who he was and decided he might be on to her. She'd have to tread even more carefully from here on in.

The elevator ride to the Palace Deck was filled with passengers wearing blue jeans, white socks, and ponytails. Nancy fit right in with them—except they were going to the Sock Hop in the disco, and Nancy was meeting Frank Hardy for a midnight swim.

The pool area was dark, and all the lights in the Olympic-size pool were turned off when Nancy lifted the latch on the fence gate and walked in.

She put down her towel, kicked off her shoes, and stuck a foot in the water. It was still warm. In the time it took to step out of her jeans and take off her sweatshirt, Nancy's eyes had adjusted to the dark. At the far end of the pool Frank was already in the water.

"Hey! I see you!" she said in a loud whisper. Then, with her arms stretched in front of her, Nancy cut cleanly into the water, hardly disturbing the surface. She swam underwater the length of the pool until she came up just inches from Frank's face.

He was swimming facedown, not moving.

"Frank Hardy, you can't fool me with that

dead man's float." Nancy laughed. "Frank? Frank?"

"Yes, Nancy. I'm right here. How's the water?" Frank asked from the deck of the pool.

Nancy froze, and her heart started thumping a thousand times a minute.

It wasn't Frank Hardy in the pool with her. It was someone else—and he was dead!

# Chapter

## Nine

Nancy wanted to scream, but when she opened her mouth, nothing came out. She was having trouble treading water. Even though she wanted to get away, she couldn't force herself to swim to the edge of the pool.

"Nancy? Are you all right?" It was Frank Hardy—the real live Frank Hardy calling to her. "Where are you? It's so dark. I can't see a thing."

"Frank," Nancy said through chattering teeth. "Come here, right away."

"Is the water cold?" Frank asked, pulling off his shirt.

"Frank," Nancy said, sounding calmer than she felt. "There's a dead body in the pool."

*Splash!* Frank dove in immediately.

A short while later Nancy was sitting on a deck chair beside the pool, wrapped in her towel, shivering. Frank's arm was around her, holding her close. Captain Helgesen was standing next to them. He had been summoned by Frank on the ship's intercom.

"It's Julio Aguerra," said the captain. He looked at the face of the corpse lying on the pool deck. "Poor devil. He was a steward. Looks like he wanted to take a midnight swim himself."

"I don't think so," Nancy said, standing up and rubbing her hair with the towel.

"He's wearing a bathing suit," Captain Helgesen said. "There are no cuts, bumps, bruises, or marks on his body. He must have been swimming and had an accident."

"Captain," Nancy said, "the other night I overheard a teenage girl and a crew person with a Spanish accent. Now a teenage girl is missing and a steward with a Spanish name is dead. We've got to suspect a connection."

The captain heaved a sigh and shook his head. "We're going to present a pretty picture to the police in Cozumel tomorrow," he said. "One corpse and one missing girl. We'd better look for some answers." Then the captain led Nancy and Frank to Julio Aguerra's cabin, where he knocked and then opened the door.

He let Nancy and Frank go inside while he stood guard.

The room was small and simple and decorated exactly like all the others they had searched earlier that day.

"You searched this cabin—didn't you?" Frank asked.

"I must have," Nancy replied. "But I don't remember it."

Nancy and Frank walked around the room, observing but not saying anything. A crucifix on the wall. Photos stuck into the dresser mirror: Julio with his arm around a couple of women, whom Nancy assumed were his sisters because of their resemblance to him. Julio in a graduate's cap and gown. Julio with a man who looked like his brother. The brother was wearing army combat clothes.

Then they found a lap-top computer and several notebooks in a desk drawer.

"What do you think he used this for?" Frank asked, looking from the computer to Nancy.

"He could have used it to look at Marcy's sample disk," Nancy said. She opened the notebooks and saw that they were filled with what appeared to be codes.

After that they searched the room even more thoroughly and carefully, being careful not to disturb anything, using pencils to lift and look under things so they wouldn't smudge whatever fingerprints might be there. They wanted to find Marcy's disk—or something to confirm that he was the contact she had met on the stairs.

After tearing apart every fixture in the room, they still found nothing. There wasn't a single computer disk anywhere.

"Would anyone really have a computer and no disks?" Nancy asked.

Frank shook his head. "Maybe they've been stolen," he said. "By the person who killed Julio."

When they had seen enough of Julio's room, Frank and Nancy went outside to report to the captain. Then they headed back to their own cabins. They desperately needed sleep.

It was late, and Nancy expected George to be asleep, but she wasn't. She was standing on her head in the middle of the room.

"Hi, George," said Nancy. "David's turned you upside down already, huh?"

"He's an absolute dream, Nancy! He's—I don't know—special somehow. It's like we're —hey, you look dead, Nancy," George said. She had brought her legs down so she could talk to Nancy.

A vision of Julio's face floated in front of Nancy's eyes.

"Where've you been?" George asked.

"Frank Hardy and I went for a swim," Nancy said.

"Sounds risky, and very romantic," George teased, raising her eyebrows. "After hours? Just the *two* of you—"

"It wasn't romantic. Believe me. We found a corpse in the swimming pool."

"Well, I'm glad you're—excuse me, but did you just say you found a *corpse* in the swimming pool?" George exclaimed, her eyes wide with shock.

"That's what I said—a corpse," Nancy said.

"Who was it?"

"A guy named Julio Aguerra."

"He's crew!" George gasped. "I mean, I *know* him! Well, not really *know* him, but, you know—I can't believe he's dead."

"We're pretty sure he was the contact for Pipeline," Nancy told her. "There was a computer in his room, but we didn't find a disk."

"Who killed him?" George asked as she sat slowly.

"You were with David all evening, right?" Nancy asked.

Suddenly George stood up again. "You don't actually think David—"

"No, but maybe one of his friends. Did you see Connor or Demetrios?"

"Huh-uh," George said, biting her lip. "Nor Gail."

Nancy shook her head. "To tell you the truth, I don't think one of them did it. I think the killer is also responsible for Marcy's disappearance."

"And that person is . . . ?" George prompted her.

Nancy shook her head and shrugged. "It looks like there's someone new in this game. Someone we didn't know about before. Maybe this person was after the disks, too, and killed Julio Aguerra to get them."

"How awful." George shivered a little.

"Anyway, someone put a note on the crew bulletin board saying the disks were still available and to leave a message in Cabin A forty-three if anyone was interested."

"And?" George said. *"Was* anyone interested?"

"Yes," Nancy said, yawning. "Someone wants to make a deal. The message said to go to the ruins in Cozumel tomorrow at noon."

"Wow! So all you have to do is show up and nab them!"

"Not so fast"—Nancy waved her off—"there's always the chance that no one will show up."

"Why not?" George asked, confused.

"Because if the message came from Julio, he can't show up. But my real guess is the message came from the person who murdered Julio," Nancy explained. "I think someone will probably be there—I just don't know *who.*"

"I wonder if Marcy's still alive," George whispered. "I mean, what do *you* think, Nancy?"

Nancy was silent for a long time. "I don't want to think about it," she said.

Early the next morning Frank, Nancy, and George met for breakfast. Joe also attended the meeting but on the run because he had to bus their table and the tables around them.

"Morning, guys. How're you doing?" Joe asked.

"Two on a scale of one to ten," Nancy said.

"We didn't have such a great night either," Joe said. "The vampire thief struck again. He got two thousand dollars from the cabin of a passenger who had just hit it big in the casino."

"How'd the thief get in?" Nancy asked.

"He used a passkey after the guy went to sleep," Joe said.

"Well, have faith in Maxwell Schweidt," Nancy said, trying to sound encouraging. "The thief has to fall for your trap sooner or later."

"I hope so," Frank said.

"Hey, look who's up early," said Joe.

The four looked over to a table on the other side of the room. Demetrios, Connor, David, and Gail were just sitting down. The three guys were talking and laughing, and only Gail looked as if something was bothering her.

"She's going to come over here as soon as she sees me," Joe said with a confident smile.

"How can you be so sure?" asked George.

"We got to know each other a little last night," said Joe, smiling at the memory of their kiss.

"Just pretend you're working, brother," Frank said. "Because you were right. Here she comes."

Gail walked over. "Hi," she said to Joe.

"Hi. Are you okay?" Joe asked.

"Yeah," Gail said. Then, to Joe's surprise, she turned away from him to talk to Nancy.

"Listen, I'm sorry I was so rotten yesterday, Nancy. Can I have breakfast with you? I've got to ask you something."

"Well, I'm on duty—" said Joe, making a graceful exit but looking and feeling a little hurt.

"What did you want to ask me?" Nancy asked.

"We've heard rumors that a body was found last night," Gail said. "Was it Marcy's?"

Nancy shook her head, and Gail's face brightened immediately. "Someone drowned last night in one of the pools," Nancy explained.

"Is it awful of me to feel relieved?" Gail asked.

Just then Joe brought their breakfast, including a Belgian waffle for Gail.

"I can't eat this. It's a thousand calories," Gail said, pushing the plate away.

"You have to," Joe said, pushing it back. "It's got your name on it."

And it did, written in maple syrup and powdered sugar. It brought a surprisingly open smile to Gail's face.

During breakfast Nancy was amazed at how unguarded Gail seemed. It was such a complete turnaround from her usual superior manner. Gail talked on and on about her college and about her friends, although Nancy noticed she was very careful not to say anything about her parents or her friends' families. It must be tough, always having to watch what you say, Nancy thought.

"So, what are you guys going to do today?" Gail finally asked.

"Me?" George said. "I have to stay on board to work. What are *you* doing, Nancy?" George asked very carefully.

"I'm getting off in Cozumel," Nancy said. "Just like ninety percent of the passengers."

"Are you going to the ruins?" Gail asked.

"Probably," Nancy said casually. Probably? Definitely! Exactly at high noon—if not earlier. But she didn't give Gail the details.

"Oh, great!" Gail said. "I am too. Maybe we can go together." She looked expectantly at Nancy.

"Gee, I'd love to, but I've got a lot of other errands to do in town," Nancy said. Like reporting Marcy's disappearance to the police. "But maybe I'll run into you somewhere. I'll keep my eyes open."

At nine o'clock that morning the ship finally docked at the island of Cozumel. Passengers eagerly lined the decks with their cameras, waiting to visit the Mexican shops, walk the sandy beaches, and ride the buses out to the ancient ruins of the Mayan civilization.

Nancy stood near the gangway, waiting to accompany Joe and the captain to police headquarters. Afterward, she and Joe would go to the ruins and try to find out who wanted to buy the CIA secrets.

But before Joe and the captain arrived, Gail came running toward Nancy. "I'm glad I found you," she said. "I can't believe it, but I think I just saw Marcy in a corridor downstairs! She started running the minute I tried to follow her. What should I do?"

"Show me," Nancy said.

Gail led the way—down stairs, through doors, down more stairs. Altogether they descended five levels, to an area of the ship where there were no cabins, only storage and equipment rooms.

"Where was she?" Nancy asked, annoyed that a lot of time had passed and Marcy was getting away.

"She went through that door!" Gail pointed.

Nancy opened the door. It was dark inside —not like a hall but like a closet. Almost immediately Nancy's internal radar went off, and she started to back away.

But it was too late. *Oof!* Pushed from behind, she stumbled forward, falling against some sort of machinery.

Then she heard the door behind her bang closed—and a dead bolt being slammed into place. She was locked in.

# Chapter

## Ten

THE LARGE EQUIPMENT CLOSET was dark, and the bitter smell of oil stung Nancy's nose. Carefully she ran her hands over the smooth metal door, searching for the doorknob.

A thousand angry questions went through her mind. And they all began with the word *why*. Why would Gail do this? Why had she trusted her? And most of all, why did she fall for such a stupid, childish trick?

When her fingers found the place where a doorknob should have been, Nancy kicked the door in frustration. The knob had been removed! Perfect, Nancy thought. She started pounding on the door with the sides of her fists.

But why was she bothering to pound? No one could possibly be around since this wasn't a passenger area. Someone had very carefully planned this.

"Help! Somebody! Open this door!" she yelled. But she couldn't hear her own screams —just the drone of what sounded like the large exhaust fans inside the closet. Even if someone were standing right outside, they probably wouldn't hear her.

Nancy had never felt more angry with herself in her life. She *knew* not to trust Gail or her friends. So why had she walked into the trap?

Because she had decided to trust her instincts, and her instincts told her that Gail wasn't so bad.

So much for instincts, Nancy thought. She kicked the door again, just to test it. Could she karate-kick it open, breaking the lock?

*"Hiiiiyahhhh!"*

Ouch—that hurt. No way. The door was heavy metal, and the lock was a solid dead bolt.

Nancy sat down on the floor in the pitch-blackness and tried to figure out what to do next. She could fish out some paper from her purse, write a note, and slip it under the door into the hallway. But it might be hours before anyone came by.

The closet was too dark for Nancy to see her watch, but she figured at least fifteen minutes had passed. The captain and Joe had probably given up waiting for her and had already gone ashore.

Just then she heard a key in the lock, and the door swung open. She blinked at the bright light and then jumped up. It was Joe!

"Joe! How did you know I was here?" Nancy asked, throwing her arms around him out of sheer surprise and relief.

"I was watching you, out of sight, up on the gangway, and I saw Gail lead you away," Joe explained. "I said to myself, something's going on. So I followed."

"Thanks," Nancy said. "Thanks a million. I owe you one."

"No problem," Joe said as they hurried up the stairs. Joe told Nancy that he couldn't believe he'd been so wrong about Gail. How could she have been so sweet and vulnerable the night before and so evil now?

"Sorry it took so long," Joe called down the stairs behind him as they went, "but I had to wait until Gail left. After she pushed you in, she hung around for a while. I guess she thought you'd get out by magic or something."

"Or something," Nancy said, laughing.

"Come on—let's find the captain. I want to get to the police."

The police were good listeners. In fact, they turned out to be better at listening than at anything else. They gave the captain their official promise to do everything they could to investigate the matter. But other than keeping an eye out for Marcy, there wasn't much they could do. More than likely, the police said, American federal agents would take charge when the ship returned to the United States.

Captain Helgesen left police headquarters looking less than satisfied. "I'll be back on board if you need me," he said. "And good luck out there. I have a feeling you'll need it."

Joe checked his watch. "Eleven o'clock," he said to Nancy. "We'd better make tracks or we'll miss the bus."

It was a bumpy, dusty ride to the ruins, and Joe and Nancy sat in silence. By the time they arrived, the sun was almost directly overhead. A visible wall of heat confronted Joe and Nancy when they stepped off the bus. The sun baked the stones and the sandy land and made shimmering images in the distance. Everything looked slightly unreal.

They took a minute to orient themselves to the plan of the crumbling walls of the Mayan buildings, which had stood there for hundreds of years.

Even with sunglasses the two detectives had to shield their eyes to look around. The first person they recognized among the other tourists was Demetrios.

He was photographing the ruins. Was this another diversion? Nancy and Joe ducked behind a portion of a stone wall and watched him from a safe distance.

After a few moments Gail appeared out of nowhere and talked with Demetrios for a minute. Then she and Demetrios went off in different directions.

"We'd better split up too," Nancy said. "I'll take Demetrios, and you take Gail. I want to keep out of her sight. If she sees me, she might get nervous and run."

"Yeah, she locked you in that closet for a reason," Joe said. "Now we're going to see what it was."

"Be careful," Nancy said as she ducked behind a stone pillar. "And remember—we're here just to *watch*."

For the next several minutes Nancy followed Demetrios, who spent the entire time photographing the ruins from every angle. She never would have guessed that he'd be so interested in the ancient architecture.

When was something going to happen, Nancy wondered. Or was it happening with Joe and Gail right then?

The sun was straight above, its heat pounding down like a hammer. Nancy took off her hat and wiped her forehead. Even wearing a cotton khaki blouse and wide-legged cotton shorts, she felt as if she were in an oven. She turned and saw another face she recognized among the twenty or so tourists climbing over the crumbling steps of an ancient temple.

It was Connor, walking down a slight incline about fifty feet away. He was wearing a baseball cap, Bermuda shorts, and a white shirt. But it was the shopping bag he was carrying that grabbed Nancy's attention. It was from Plummer's!

They're using that for the signal again, Nancy thought, stepping out of sight to make sure Connor wouldn't spot her.

So it was Connor who had put the note on the bulletin board. He had the disks in that bag, and he was waiting. "Noon. Alone. *I'll* find *you*."

But when Nancy stepped out again to double-check, Connor had disappeared in the shimmering heat. Had he been just a mirage? She quickly started walking down the incline, trying to spot him.

Suddenly she was cut off by a large group. Nancy dodged, cutting through the crowd. There he was! He was moving very quickly just ahead of her. She kept catching glimpses of him as he walked, looking expectantly at every face he passed.

"Noon. Alone. *I'll* find *you.*"

He's trying to pretend he's got everything under control, Nancy thought. But he doesn't know who he's waiting for, and he's a sitting duck out here.

"Take your picture, señorita?"

Nancy looked down at a Mexican boy with an instant camera. He was about ten years old, the same age as his battered camera. He had a small sombrero, a red bandanna around his neck, and he was wearing a Bruce Springsteen T-shirt.

Nancy shook her head and tried to keep her eyes on Connor.

"But you are so beautiful, and the ruins are so beautiful," said the boy. "Only two dollars."

Nancy said, "Not today," and kept walking.

"Maybe a map? Also two dollars. Very good map—"

"Map?" The word triggered an idea. All along, Nancy had assumed that after the transaction, whoever bought the disks would reboard the *Duchess*—and that the authorities would be waiting on the dock in Miami to arrest him.

But now her heart began beating faster as she considered a different scenario. What would stop the buyer from taking the disks and forgetting about the ship? He could run anywhere. That would be the worst possible scenario, because then there would be no way for Nancy to prove anything. And they'd *never* find Marcy!

Nancy hurried toward Connor, but he kept getting farther away. The two of them were circling the ruins, she realized. She felt as if she were moving in slow motion through the thick heat.

Forget catching the buyer, Nancy decided. Forget watching the deal go down. All she wanted to do now was to stop Connor and destroy the disks before the American secrets were traded away.

"You can take a picture of me for a dollar," said the little boy, running in front of Nancy.

"No. Please stop following me," she said. Connor was outpacing her. She had to get to him. But there were too many walls in front of her, walls of rock and walls of heat. Nancy was feeling faint from the extreme temperature. Her face was beaded with moisture. Why didn't Connor have enough sense to stand in one place? She lost him and found him again. Where was Joe?

Suddenly there were sirens and clouds of dust in the air as two police cars drove up to the ruins and stopped abruptly. Uniformed officers and a man in a suit got out of the cars. They were running in Nancy's direction!

She stood stock-still as they passed her and ran up the path straight to Connor. Then they took him by the arm and led him back to their cars, past the stunned tourists now gathering around. Nancy tried to run after them, but the crowds got in her way. And just as she finally got to the cars, they were driven off.

"What happened?" she asked the people who were standing nearest the spot where the cars had been. "What did the police want?"

A gray-haired woman with red sunglasses said, "You should have seen it. It was pretty exciting. Just like on television."

"What did they say?" Nancy asked.

"They said they needed him to come with them immediately," the old woman said.

"But why?" Nancy asked.

"To identify a body!" the woman announced. "They said the body of a young girl washed ashore and they think he might know who it is. Never a dull moment, eh?"

Nancy's heart sank. The body had to be Marcy's.

In her mind Nancy pictured the other four when they heard the news. And they thought they could handle everything themselves—now they were really going to have to show what they could handle.

"Señorita! Señorita!" The boy was back. "He wants to see you."

"Who?"

"Follow me. Hurry!" the boy said, already in motion up the hill.

"Is it Joe? Is something wrong?" Nancy called to the short figure leading her toward the remains of an ancient building.

"Follow me! I will take you!"

Nancy was even hotter and more out of breath when she caught up with the boy. She leaned a hand against the rough stone of the wall of what used to be a room in a temple. The walls were all that was left in most places, and they formed a sort of maze, or labyrinth. Between the walls were dusty and empty spaces.

"There's no one here," she panted.

The boy looked at her and ran around the corner and back down the hill.

"Hey!" Nancy called. But she didn't have the energy to follow him. "Joe. Are you in there?" she asked. She wiped her forehead and took a couple of deep breaths. "Come on, Joe. This is a bad time for playing games." She was so thirsty she would have traded all her money for a drink of water. She walked along the wall. Small stones crunched under her feet. "Joe?" she called. She stopped again.

This time she heard stones crunching under someone else's feet. Nancy was quiet. The other footsteps stopped. Were they inside the building? Around the other side? Nancy turned to walk the other way.

Suddenly from behind, someone grabbed her! As she struggled to free herself, a hand covered her mouth. There was a cloth in the hand.

Then she smelled the unmistakable odor of chloroform. Her vision blurred and the room spun.

Now she was no longer fighting. She was falling. . . .

Nancy was unconscious even before she hit the ground.

# Chapter

## Eleven

FRANK HARDY started pacing the deck again. All day he'd been taking pictures and assuming his beeper would go off at any minute. The waiting was driving him crazy.

Then in an instant the waiting was over. The beeper in his pocket was sounding.

Frank broke into a sprint. Forget the elevator. He had to go down two levels, fast. He leapt down the stairs, three and four at a time, sliding around the corners. Finally he reached the long hallway and ran toward Maxwell Schweidt's room.

The door was still ajar when he got there.

Panting, Frank stood for a moment deciding what to do. He could wait for the thief to finish and walk out red-handed. Or he could push the door open and kick off a surprise party.

Frank had been waiting too long for this moment. He kicked the door open and jumped into the room, ready to strike.

But the room was empty.

"Impossible!" Frank yelled in frustration. *No one* could burglarize a cabin that fast!

Quickly he checked the drawers and closets. Nothing had been moved, nothing had been taken, nothing had been touched—except the dresser mirror. There Frank found a short and taunting note written in what looked like black crayon. It said:

Maxwell Schweidt doesn't exist. But *I* do! And you'll never catch me!

Frank closed the door in frustration and made his way to the Paradise Lounge to check out one of his suspects, Rick, the bartender. Without passengers the *Duchess* was like a ghost ship.

Rick was behind the bar, cleaning up and straightening bottles. To Frank's surprise, he saw George there too.

"Hey, Rick, how about a ginger ale?" Frank

asked. As Rick moved to the other end of the bar to talk to Wendy Larson, a beautiful blackjack dealer, Frank whispered to George, "How long have you been talking to Rick?"

"About fifteen or twenty minutes," George answered. "Why?"

"The alarm went off, but it was a joke. The thief knows Maxwell Schweidt doesn't exist," Frank said.

"Well, it couldn't have been Rick," George said. "He's been talking my ear off. It's an occupational hazard."

Frank frowned and eyed Rick carefully. But George was right—there was no way Rick could be in two places at once.

"Okay," Frank said. "Do me a favor. Go find Chef Borka in the kitchen. See if he has an alibi for the past half hour. I'll go check on Esteban. He's been reassigned to the men's locker room." Grinning, he walked out. "Save that soda for me, Rick," he called over his shoulder.

It was nearly six o'clock when George met Frank again on the Princess Deck, watching the passengers return from the Mayan ruins.

"Are Nancy and Joe back?"

"I don't know," Frank said. "I just got here."

"I've got good news," George said. "Chef Borka has been slicing onions for his famous quiche Marjorie for hours."

Frank didn't say anything.

"Hey, don't you know good news when you hear it?" she said. "If it's not Rick, and it's not Borka, then it has to be Esteban!"

"It's not Esteban. He's been in sick bay all day," Frank said. "The nurse said he hasn't moved from his bed."

"Uh-oh," George said sympathetically. "Back to square one, huh?"

"Yeah," Frank said, frustration written all over his face.

Another bus pulled up at the dock. The tourists were returning, dustier, hotter, and poorer than when they left. Each busload of passengers brought straw hats and piñatas, colorful shirts, and lots of film to be developed. But they didn't bring Nancy.

"I don't see her, do you?" George said, leaning over the railing.

"No, but I do see Joe," Frank said. "He's got his arm around Gail."

Frank and George watched Joe for a minute and realized that something was wrong with Gail. She was stumbling and having a hard time walking. "Let's get down there," Frank said.

They worked their way down the gangplank and met Joe and Gail halfway up.

"What happened?" Frank asked his brother. "Is she hurt?"

"No, she's upset," Joe said. He pulled Frank and George aside. "The police found Marcy's body washed ashore," he continued in a low voice. "Connor and Gail tried to identify it, but—" Joe shook his head quickly to stop either of them from asking for details.

Frank and George didn't need Joe to draw them a picture. They could see Gail's blotchy, tear-stained face and figure out the rest.

"Where's Nancy?" George asked, taking Joe aside when they reached the top of the gangplank.

"Isn't she back yet?" Joe asked. He looked startled when Frank shook his head. "How about Demetrios? We agreed that Nancy would stick close to him."

"I haven't seen him either," Frank said.

Joe looked worried.

"Gail's really freaked out. I'm going to walk her to her cabin and then report the bad news about Marcy to the captain. Let me know when Nancy shows up."

Frank nodded. "And when you get a chance, check out Cabin E two-seventeen," he muttered. "We struck out."

* * *

Frank and George waited for an hour while the remaining passengers straggled back onto the ship. Eventually Joe returned to stand watch with them. Nancy still hadn't checked in.

As a group of people came on board, a man pulled Frank aside and slipped him five dollars. Frank had noticed the man before—he always wore a black knit shirt, even on the hottest afternoons. "Something funny was going on out there, wasn't it?" the man asked.

"What do you mean?" Frank asked.

"We heard stories," the man said.

"What stories?" Frank asked.

The man spoke more softly. "You know, about a body washing up," he said. "We heard that a passenger on this ship fell over and washed up on Cozumel."

"I don't know anything," Frank said.

The man handed him another five. "Find out." He smiled and walked away.

Frank turned back to his brother and George. "Who was that?" Frank asked.

"I don't know," Joe said.

Frank handed him a five-dollar bill. "Find out," he said.

Connor arrived in a police car a few minutes later and climbed the gangplank. He headed straight inside without saying a word. He looked numb.

Then David and Demetrios pulled up in a taxi. They, too, looked as though they'd heard the news about Marcy.

"Something's wrong," said Frank, his warm brown eyes full of worry. "Demetrios is back, and Nancy's not tailing him. I'm going to look for her."

"I'll come with you. We can't leave her in Cozumel," George said.

"I'll tell the captain to keep the gangplank down," said Joe.

"Good idea! Let's go!" said George.

When she came to, Nancy was someplace she had never seen before. Someplace dark. Someplace dusty. Her arms and legs tingled. She felt dirty, and a hundred scratches and cuts covered her body. She knew she must have been dragged wherever she was before being left in a heap.

She wanted to move, but she couldn't because the chloroform was still working in her body. The feeling was just coming back into her arms and legs, which lay bent in awkward positions.

She tried to think back. The young Mexican boy . . . The smell of chloroform . . . But who had drugged her? She had seen no one and remembered nothing.

It was so dark. Gradually her eyes were

focusing and adjusting. That was when she saw the wall—she was in a large cave. There was no sound except for water dripping somewhere in the distance. "Hello!" she shouted, but the only reply was her voice echoing emptily.

Suddenly something flew high above her. A bat! Before Nancy could recover from her shock, there was a loud rustle and the screech of a thousand little voices.

Now many more bats had joined the one, whizzing high above her.

How would she ever get out of there?

# Chapter

## Twelve

STAY CALM, Nancy told herself. Think. It was hard to do with her mind still fuzzy from the chloroform.

Whoever had dragged her into the cave wouldn't have brought her in very far. People are very heavy when unconscious, she knew. She had probably been pulled only far enough so she'd feel lost.

And lost she was. She might as well have been miles from the entrance.

Suddenly another flight of bats whizzed by her, fluttering and screeching. Nancy's heart was in her throat.

That's it! she realized. The bats! It must be dusk, and they were heading outside to begin their nightly search for food. All she had to do was follow them and they'd lead her to the entrance.

It was hard to tell which way they were going with all the echoes in the cave. But as flight after flight flew by her, she finally found the entrance. The moon was just rising in the east. And there, in the distance, was a narrow ribbon of road, and off to the right, the Mayan ruins.

Now to get back to the ship. It was a long walk to El Pueblo, the village outside the ruins, but she had to get there.

After walking awhile—had five minutes passed, or fifty?—two lights bobbed on the horizon. They looked like stars racing side by side across the deserted landscape. A minute later Nancy recognized them as headlights of a car.

The driver braked to a dusty stop when he saw Nancy waving her arms in the beam of the headlights.

There were two police officers in the car. The young one drove, and the older man, with an unlighted cigar in his mouth, rode next to him.

"Señorita Drew?" asked the older officer, sticking his head out of the window. The cigar moved from one side of his mouth to the other as he talked.

"Yes, that's me," Nancy said, approaching the car.

"Captain Helgesen phoned to say that you had been left," he said, stepping out of the car to open the back door for her.

"Thank goodness." Nancy fell more than stepped into the back of the car.

"You missed your boat, señorita," said the young officer, spinning the car around and driving quickly back toward the village.

The older officer turned around and handed Nancy a bottle of water.

"Oh, thank you," Nancy said, appreciatively taking it.

"It's not such a good day for your captain either, señorita," the older officer said. "First one of his passengers floats ashore, and then one of them is left behind."

"The body was identified?" Nancy asked.

"Not positively," the young officer said.

"Well, how can I rejoin the ship?" Nancy asked.

"Don't worry. We'll have you there in no time, especially the way Manuel drives." The older officer chuckled.

But in El Pueblo Nancy learned that the police did not have a boat available immediately. They were trying to locate an available shore patrol boat in one of the larger ports on the mainland of Mexico. It could take hours.

While she waited, Nancy stepped outside into the cool night air. As she leaned against the brick wall, a child with a red bandanna walked by.

"Hey, you!" Nancy shouted. It was the boy with the camera, the one who had led her up the hill to the place where she had been attacked! If she could catch him, maybe she could find out who had sent him.

The boy looked at Nancy, his eyes wide with terror. Then he took off, running at full speed. Nancy followed as fast as she could, but he had the advantage of knowing every twist and turn of the alleys. Nancy lost him by the waterfront. Giving up, she leaned against a dock to catch her breath.

It was a well-lighted area, with boats bobbing quietly on their moorings. Nancy saw that an old man had stopped scrubbing down his small fishing boat to watch her.

"Did you see a young kid go by here?" Nancy asked.

The old man ran his hand over his bald head. He didn't say anything.

*"Vio un niño, muy rapido?"* Nancy said. She spoke Spanish perfectly well, so why wasn't he answering her now?

She decided to take another approach.

"Nice boat," she said. *"Barco muy lindo."*

*"Sí,"* the man said proudly. "Is good boat. Very good."

So he did speak English! "I have money," Nancy told him, speaking slowly and carefully. "Can you take me out to a cruise ship?"

*"Sí,"* said the old man with a laugh. He extended his arm to help Nancy aboard. She'd have to radio the police from the ship and tell them she got a lift—if she ever got there!

The old man started the small engine and steered the boat out of the harbor. Nancy sat on deck and watched the stars dance to the rolling movement of the craft. She didn't know when, but she fell asleep. Sometime later, when the old man woke her up, she was covered with a blanket.

"Señorita," he said, pointing to the *Duchess* in the distance. It glowed in the night like a comet on the water.

A half hour later Nancy was sitting in Captain Helgesen's office.

"This is the second time I've had to drop rescue boats on this cruise," the captain complained. "Do you see all the trouble one passenger being late can make?"

"Captain, I wasn't just late," Nancy explained. "I was drugged and left for dead. But I think I found out who's been trying to sell the disks."

The captain waved his hands to cut her off. "I don't want to know what you've learned," he said. "While you were away I heard from the CIA. They gave me a very short message—*hands off!* According to the agency, all five of those crazy kids do have access to top-level CIA secrets. My orders are clear—sail home and do nothing to alarm them. The CIA will meet the ship in Miami."

"Captain, it's too late for not alarming them," Nancy said. "Someone killed Marcy—someone killed Julio—and someone tried to kill me. Shutting me down is not going to guarantee you a peaceful trip home."

"Ms. Drew," the captain said, standing up quickly and pacing his office. "I appreciate all you're doing, really I do. But I hope you won't be offended if I suggest that on your next vacation, you fly the Concorde instead!"

They stared at each other for a moment and then burst into laughter.

"Sorry," he said. "You have stuck your neck out pretty far already, haven't you? I don't know what you and Frank and Joe think you can do. But if you can put a stop to this, and do it quietly, I'll go along with you. I don't relish making headlines as the skipper of a spy boat."

Nancy left the captain's office and hurried off to find George.

"Nancy," George cried happily from the

ballroom. She was wearing a hand-embroidered Mexican dress for the fiesta, which was in full swing. Passengers were crowding around George as she handed out party favors from a large wicker basket.

"Later," Nancy called with a smile to her busy friend.

Nancy couldn't immediately find Frank and Joe, so she went back to her cabin to clean up and sleep.

A hot shower made her feel human again. Then she slipped into a nightgown and sat on her bed, her mind whirling.

Switching off her light, Nancy snuggled into bed, ready for a long night's rest.

"What the—" Nancy was shocked out of her drowsy state by something brushing against her hand.

Fully awake now, Nancy threw back the covers. There beside her was a large and deadly-looking scorpion!

# Chapter

## Thirteen

NANCY LOOKED AROUND for something, anything, to protect herself with. Any second now the scorpion would strike. Nancy had to kill it before it killed her!

In her peripheral vision Nancy spotted the phone on the bedside table. With her right hand she slowly reached out for it. Sweat was pouring down her forehead, stinging her eyes. As the scorpion thrashed its tail, ready to strike, she inched her hand toward the phone, lifted the handset, and swiftly brought it down on the creature with a crunch.

When she was sure it was dead, Nancy threw on her robe and let herself out of the room, her heart beating a mile a minute. "Got to find Frank and Joe," she said out loud as she ran down the corridor to their cabin.

Frank and Joe had just returned to their room.

"Nancy!" cried Frank. "George and I got off the ship to search for you, but the captain gave us only an hour. He said the police would be able to find you more easily."

"I understand," she said, smiling at the brothers. Nancy suddenly felt weak in the knees and sat down on one of the beds.

"What's happened? Are you all right?" Frank asked.

"I'm achy and stiff," Nancy said. "Actually I don't feel too bad considering the chloroform, the bats, and the scorpion."

"What?" Joe asked. "What happened at the ruins? When I lost track of you, I thought you'd gone back."

"I know," Nancy said. Then she told her friends everything that had happened. She finished by telling them that Connor had the disks.

"First chloroform and now a scorpion in your bed. It's probably the same guy," Joe said. "But who?"

Nancy shrugged. "I think it's got to be the same person who murdered Julio."

The mood in the room was somber, as

Nancy's friends understood that someone had really tried to do away with her.

"Let's go talk to Connor," Joe said, standing up suddenly.

"We've done enough talking," Nancy said. The Hardys could hear the change of attitude in her voice. It was a get-tough sound. "I want to find the disks and stop this thing cold."

"Shouldn't you be on the sidelines until you get back in shape?" Frank asked, concerned.

Nancy just looked at Frank, and he knew she had no intention of being benched. "I want you guys to make sure Connor is out of his cabin for a while tomorrow after dinner. Or is it *tonight* after dinner—it's so late. Then call me and tell me so I can search it," she said.

"Sounds okay to me," Frank said. As he placed his passkey in her palm, he let his hand linger in hers a moment longer than necessary.

"What if she doesn't find the disks?" Joe asked.

"Bad news," said Frank. "Because it probably means Connor sold them." His face clouded over, and Nancy knew he was worried about her. Real people were getting hurt.

Nancy returned to her cabin for a good night's sleep.

At dinner the next night in the dining room, George stepped up to the microphone and greeted the passengers. She was wearing a gypsy fortune-teller costume, and Frank and Joe were dressed as gorillas.

"Tonight before our Masquerade Ball, we have a special treat for you," she said. "Please welcome, the one, the only, the Great Lantoni!"

There was a burst of music and then, as the lights dimmed, a puff of white smoke. A moment later the Great Lantoni, a short, chubby magician, appeared on the stage.

"Good evening, ladies and gentlemen. It's a pleasure for you to see me tonight," said the Great Lantoni. "To perform my magic for you, however, I will need an assistant. Who would like to volunteer?"

Hands went up all over the large room.

"No, no, no. Too eager. You've probably seen the tricks before." The Great Lantoni smiled. He stepped down off the stage and wandered among the guests. "I would like a different volunteer—you, young sir!"

The Great Lantoni was pointing right at Connor. He, Gail, and Demetrios were the only people in the room not wearing costumes.

"No way," Connor said.

"He wants to be encouraged!" the Great Lantoni cried. As soon as they heard that, the guests burst into applause. Even Gail started encouraging Connor to go up on the stage. When Lantoni grabbed him by the arm, Connor gave in.

Joe and Frank had instructed the Great Lantoni well.

Joe waited until he knew Connor was trapped. Then he went to a telephone and dialed Nancy's cabin. "All clear," he said, and hung up.

Nancy didn't waste a second. Dressed in her masquerade costume, she slipped out of her room to head for Connor's cabin.

There were people in the corridor as Nancy reached the cabin, but she didn't flinch. She put the passkey in the door confidently, as if she were going into her own room.

Nancy turned the key and pushed against the door, but it opened only slightly. She pushed again. Something was blocking the door, keeping her from opening it.

"Hey, I love your hat," said a voice behind her.

Nancy closed the door quickly and turned around. There was a young man with half his face grease-painted white and the other half black—exactly like the colors of his harlequin costume. He looked like Nancy's twin. He reached out and jingled the bells on her floppy cap.

"How about you and me going to the dance and making fools of ourselves?" said the harlequin with a grin.

You've got a head start, Nancy thought, hoping he'd just disappear and fast. But he leaned against the wall as if he planned to stay there all night.

Nancy realized the only way to get rid of him was to say yes. "Okay, I'll meet you," Nancy said. "Where?"

"I'll be up on the Palace Deck, pushing people into the pool," he said.

"I'm counting the moments," Nancy said, watching him walk down the hall. Then she turned and tried to open the door again.

The next time she gave it all the muscle she had. And whatever was blocking the door moved just enough so that she could squeeze into the room.

But when she got inside, her heart started pounding and she felt faint. Now she saw why the door wouldn't open.

There was a body lying on the floor!

# Chapter

## Fourteen

**N**ANCY LOOKED CAREFULLY and saw that it was David! She knew she shouldn't move him, but she had to know how hurt he was.

She knelt down and pressed her fingers firmly against his neck. Nancy exhaled loudly, not realizing she had been holding her breath. She could feel his pulse—he was still alive. Then she ran to the telephone to call the ship's doctor.

"There's been an accident in Cabin E fifty," she reported. "A man is unconscious. Please come immediately."

After the doctor had hung up, Nancy continued to stand holding the telephone and look-ing at David.

What was he doing in here, she wondered. Was he meeting another spy? Was he working with Connor to sell his country's secrets? Looking at David's innocent face, it seemed hard to believe. And yet . . .

The doctor arrived quickly. He was a cool, handsome man with silver hair, who con-ducted his examination without much talk.

"Is it bad?" Nancy asked. The doctor grunted an answer, but Nancy didn't want to press him for more information just then.

David moaned and opened his eyes. He looked at the doctor, and suddenly his face became fearful.

"I'm the ship's doctor. Don't worry, young man," said the doctor.

"David," Nancy said.

David was groggy, but he smiled when he recognized her voice. He still looked confused, though.

"It's Nancy," she went on. "Connor's door was open, and I found you in here. Can you tell me what happened?"

"I came in to borrow a sweater from Connor —he said I could. Someone was in here. He spun me around and hit me on the head."

Nancy looked around the room. Hit him with what? There was nothing heavy nearby.

Nothing had been dropped, and nothing seemed out of place.

"David, did you see anything? Anything at all?" Nancy asked.

David tried to sit up, but the doctor pushed him down again.

"Slight concussion," the doctor said as he walked to the telephone to call for a stretcher.

"Where's Connor?" David asked, looking around the room. "Tell Connor."

"Tell Connor what?" Nancy asked, kneeling beside him. His eyes told her that his mind was going in and out of focus.

"Connor's my buddy," David mumbled. "We always help each other out."

"David, I'm your friend too," Nancy said, "and I want to help you. You've got to tell me what happened."

"You're not Connor," he said. "Connor doesn't like you."

"Maybe not. But Connor doesn't know me, does he?" Nancy said. "If he knew me, he might not be so suspicious. David, you've got to tell me: Are you and Connor doing something that you shouldn't?"

David looked at Nancy and noticed her costume. "Dressed for the prom?" he asked.

"Please be serious. And try to remember," Nancy said.

"I didn't see anything. The room was dark.

Then—kablooie!" David paused, a funny look on his face. "I didn't see anything, but I smelled something."

"What do you mean?" Nancy asked, taking his hand.

"Pipe tobacco," he said. He was remembering clearly now. "I was lying down. Someone bent over me. Pieces of loose tobacco fell on my face. Smelled sweet but strange." He winced, perhaps as he remembered being struck.

Nancy looked around the rug where David had been lying. She picked up a couple of strands of tobacco from the rug.

"David," Nancy said, "maybe you were robbed. Did you have any money on you? Or did Connor keep some in the room?"

"Connor doesn't believe in carrying money," David said. "But I've got some in my pocket."

Nancy checked quickly. "It's still there. You weren't robbed. Then what was that guy doing in here?"

David shook his head, and his eyes started to close. His mind was drifting again. "Where's Connor?" he mumbled. "And Gail? And Demetrios? And Marcy?"

After David was taken to the sick bay, Nancy searched the cabin thoroughly—in dresser drawers and suitcase linings, inside the toilet tank, behind the paintings, between the mattresses—anyplace that anyone could hide something flat like computer disks. It didn't take long for her to see that someone had already searched the cabin before her. And that probably meant one thing: She was too late to find the disks. Someone had beaten her to them!

Now what, Nancy wondered. Now it didn't matter how many people were in on the plot, because the disks were gone. And the *X* factor —the unknown player who had killed Julio and Marcy and conked David—probably had them.

Unless—

Unless Connor had hidden the disks so well that *no one* could find them.

Nancy felt like confronting Connor, having it out, face-to-face. But she knew he'd deny hiding the disks, and his friends would back him up. In the end she'd be no closer to catching anyone.

She went to the ballroom, looking for George or Frank or Joe. Costumed people were dancing in long snakelike lines, holding on to one another's waists. The music thumped and drowned out all conversation. Confetti and streamers were everywhere.

Nancy wove her way through the twisting, shouting crowds and finally caught a glimpse of a gorilla. She knew Frank and Joe were both wearing gorilla costumes, but this gorilla had to be Frank because he was taking pictures of people in their costumes by a fake palm tree.

"Frank," she called.

Frank lowered his camera and looked at Nancy. "How did it go?"

Nancy shook her head.

"Come on," said a man dressed like a rooster. "Take the picture. Take the picture."

"I can't talk now," Frank told Nancy. "Joe and I will meet you at nine in Maxwell's cabin."

Later that night Nancy, Frank, and Joe met in the privacy of Maxwell Schweidt's cabin. Nancy told them about finding David and about the missing disks.

"Here's an interesting thought," Joe said. "When David tells Connor that you were in his room, Connor will think *you've* got the disks."

"Just what I need." Nancy groaned. Then she looked up at the letters of the message still written on the mirror.

"Listen, I've got an idea how to trap Connor," Frank said. "But it'll work only if the disks really have been stolen."

Nancy turned to face him.

"What is it?" she asked.

"We slip Connor a note saying something

like 'I have the disks. Do you want the money? You know what room to look in.' And we don't sign it, of course. If the disks are missing, he'll come right to Cabin A forty-three."

"And we'll be waiting here," Nancy said with a smile.

"Sounds good," Joe said. "Just by walking in, he'll be saying he knows about A forty-three and he knows what disks we mean. That's half his confession right there!"

"It's worth a try," Nancy said. "I'll write the note. Does Maxwell Schweidt have paper and a pencil in here?" She began searching through the dresser drawers, but then she stopped. All of a sudden she looked up at the vanity mirror where the taunting message to Frank had been written by the thief. "Hey, I thought you said this message was written in black crayon," Nancy said, smudging a word with her finger.

"So?" Frank answered.

"It's not," Nancy said with a smile. "It's eyeliner pencil. I hate to tell you this, guys, but I think your cabin thief is a woman!"

# Chapter

## Fifteen

EYELINER? The cabin thief's a woman? You're joking, right?" Joe said.

Nancy said nothing. She just looked in her purse for a moment and removed an eyeliner pencil. Then she wrote, "Ha-ha, some joke" on the mirror.

Frank was angry at himself as he stared at the two messages on the glass. "She's right about the pencil. We've been complete bozos not to follow up on the women crew members!"

Joe was not as quick to admit the mistake. "But don't forget, Lillian Hallock said she saw a *man*," he said.

"She saw someone in a white crew uniform, with dark hair and a vampire face," Frank said. "Underneath that mask there could have been a springer spaniel for all we know. Besides, maybe we've been bozos twice. Maybe it's a woman—with a male accomplice."

"Okay, okay," Joe said. "I'm a bozo. I'm going out right now to buy a red nose. Now what?"

"I hate to do this to you, Nancy," Frank said. "But this may be the break we need. Could you go on hold—give Joe and me half an hour to get back on track with this case? Then we'll meet you in A forty-three at ten o'clock, ready to clobber Connor."

"Okay," Nancy said. "I'll write the note to him, but I won't slip it under his door until you're ready."

Ten minutes later Frank and Joe were holding a printout of the female crew members who were on break when Lillian Hallock's cabin was robbed. They paced the deck while they talked.

"This list is a killer," Frank said, looking at the twenty names. "But fortunately you've flirted with most of these women. Any good suspects, Joe?"

"Sorry, none of them ever mentioned being the ship's thief." Joe shrugged playfully.

As they were passing the bar at the gambling casino entrance, they heard a conversation in progress.

"Yes, sir, Rick, I just won five beans at blackjack—that's five *thousand* dollars!" a man with a Texas accent was saying.

Joe poked his brother. "Why doesn't he just take out an ad in the personals? 'Rich man looking for thief to steal his money.'"

Frank carefully watched the faces of the crew members, who were listening to this conversation. They seemed amused but not particularly interested.

"Rick," the Texan said, "I believe I should be going off to bed. Here's a hundred dollars. You're a good man."

Rick refused the money. "Good night, Mr. Robbins," he said with a smile, handing the money back.

Frank and Joe followed the Texan back to his cabin. They wanted to make sure he made it all right, and they wanted to talk to him.

"Mr. Robbins," Frank said outside the man's cabin, "wouldn't you sleep better if you put your money in the ship's safe?"

"No, thanks," the man said. "I can take care of myself." He put his key in his cabin door and walked inside. He closed the door, and Frank and Joe could hear the click of the lock.

"I'm going to stick around—at least for a few minutes," Joe said. "I have the feeling it's going to be worth my time."

"Okay, but what about Nancy? She's waiting for us in A forty-three, so we can snag Connor," Frank said.

Nancy *was* sitting in the dark in Cabin A forty-three, the cabin they had been calling the mailbox. Footsteps passed. She had folded and unfolded and refolded her note to Connor a hundred times. She opened it and read it again.

"I have your disks. If you want your money, you know what cabin to look in."

It was unsigned, of course.

Finally a key scraped in the lock, and Frank Hardy appeared in the doorway. He had gotten rid of his gorilla costume and was again wearing his ship's uniform. Nancy, too, had changed back to street clothes.

He flipped a light on with his elbow as he came in, carrying a tray of food and coffee, a deck of cards, and a book of crossword puzzles, which he set on the dresser.

"It could be a long night," he said. "Although I doubt if we'll get bored enough to need these." He smiled as he tossed the book of crossword puzzles into Nancy's lap.

"Probably not," Nancy agreed. "Well, I'm off." Now that Frank was back, she was anxious to slip the note under Connor's door.

Frank was sitting on the floor, watching the door, when Nancy got back. The room was almost completely dark, except for one small night-light.

"Now we wait," he said, munching a ham sandwich. "Want one?"

"No, thanks," said Nancy, watching him eat the sandwich. "Well, okay, maybe a bite." Frank leaned over and offered her some.

"Thanks," said Nancy, gulping the food down. His brown eyes were so warm, so friendly, Nancy couldn't help smiling at him. Frank's girlfriend, Callie, really was a lucky girl.

"You know, Nancy," he started to say. "Sometimes I wonder—"

But he stopped and held his breath. Someone was at the door—the knob turned, and the door swung open slowly.

"Am I late?" asked Joe Hardy, walking in.

"Right on time," Frank said with a relieved laugh. "Why are you back so soon? You were gone only ten minutes."

"Well, the Texan is snoring peacefully, and no one came by. I decided I'd be wasting my time there. And I knew you'd be lonely without me," he said.

An hour passed. The food disappeared, the

coffee got cold, and the crossword puzzles got too hard.

Then, at about one A.M., the rattle of metal against metal made Frank, Nancy, and Joe jump up. It didn't sound like a key, but whatever it was, it was doing the job of opening the lock. Frank and Joe moved closer to the door. It swung open, and there was Connor.

He looked in, and for one instant his eyes registered surprise. Then he realized he had been trapped, and he took off, running.

But Frank and Joe were already airborne. Frank caught him by the shoulders, and Joe tackled him at the legs. The three of them collapsed in the hallway, a struggling mass of arms and legs.

When they stood up, however, Joe had Connor's arm twisted behind his back. He pushed Connor into the cabin, and Frank quickly slammed the door and locked it.

"What's this about?" Connor asked angrily as soon as he caught his breath.

"What do you think?" Nancy said calmly.

"I've got nothing to talk about," Connor replied as icily.

"Connor, the CIA knows what's happening. They're going to meet the ship in Miami," Nancy said. "So if you don't help us find the disks, all they have is you. And you know better than we do what that means."

Connor tried to stare blankly at her as though none of what she had said meant anything to him. But Nancy could see that he was struggling to keep his fear from showing.

"This is what I know," Nancy went on. "I know you're all CIA kids, and I know Marcy was Pipeline and you were helping her. And I think she disappeared right after she met the steward Julio Aguerra on the stairs, because no one saw her after that—until you identified her in Cozumel."

Connor closed his eyes, presumably to blot out the memory of Marcy's body. They could see on his face how horrible it had been. When he opened his eyes, it was clear that he was ready to talk.

"Whose idea was it to sell the disks?" Joe asked.

"Marcy's," Connor said finally. He was choosing his words carefully, telling them only what he thought they needed to know.

"You mean one day she just woke up and said, 'I think I'll sell some CIA secrets today'?" Joe asked.

"Marcy never did anything impulsively," Connor said. "Everything was planned."

"So why did she do it?" Nancy asked impatiently.

"She wanted to ruin her father," Connor said, staring at Nancy. "She hated him for never being home. Not even when her mother died. She told me she could get his secrets, all kinds of stuff about what he was doing in Central America. And she wanted to do something big with it, something that would really embarrass him and destroy his career.

"I tried to talk her out of it," Connor went on, "but she was determined. She was going to do it, with me or without me. So"—he shook his head and laughed bitterly—"so I went along with her to make sure she didn't get hurt."

Nancy, Frank, and Joe were quiet, waiting for Connor to continue.

"Anyway," he said, "I got a message onto a computer in an embassy in Central America. I told them we had secret information about $X$, $Y$, and $Z$. It's better if the three of you don't know the exact details. I told the embassy if they were interested in buying the secrets, we'd be in touch. Marcy set up all the rules. She picked the cruise and told them to put an agent on the boat. Everything was her idea—calling herself Pipeline, the shopping bag from Plummer's, the stairs at nine o'clock."

"Why weren't you at the six A.M. meeting on the Princess Deck?" Nancy asked.

Connor looked puzzled. "What meeting? I didn't know about it," he said. "Marcy said, 'It's set.' That's all. I didn't know anything about where or when."

"And you put a note on the crew's bulletin board because you thought she had been kidnapped?" Frank said, prompting Connor to go on.

Connor wiped his forehead with his sleeve and leaned against a dresser. "All I knew was that her contact worked on the ship. I thought if I gave him the disks, he'd let Marcy go. I thought she was still alive. Then he sent me a note, arranging a meeting at the ruins," Connor said.

"No, I don't think Marcy's contact sent you that note," Nancy said. "Her contact was Julio Aguerra, a steward. Frank and I found him dead in a swimming pool. Someone else had to have been watching you from the beginning— and that someone wrote you the note. Now this guy's stolen your disks, and we don't have a clue about him."

"When I saw Marcy's body . . ." Connor couldn't say anything for a moment. "The whole time I really thought she was still alive. I thought I could pull this off and get her back. When I knew she was dead, I decided not to sell the disks."

"Oh, sure," Nancy said. "That's why you

ran in here to get your money when I sent you that note."

"I only wanted to know who it was," Connor insisted.

"Don't we all," Frank said. "You know, two people have died and two others have gotten hurt because you and your friends are running around playing spy—and you don't even know who you're dealing with!"

"Listen, you don't understand. My friends don't know a thing about this."

"Right," Joe said. "Then why did Gail lock Nancy in the storage closet?"

"I didn't tell her why. I just asked her to do it for me, and she did. That's the way we are."

Nancy thought of David lying in the ship's hospital with a concussion. Then she remembered something else. "We do know one thing about this agent," she said. "He smokes a pipe."

"Oh?" Connor murmured, his face falling.

"David said the tobacco was very unusual," Frank said.

"Oh, no," Connor moaned. He started rubbing his temples and pacing the room. "That's bad—very bad—"

"What's going on?" Joe asked.

"We're dead," Connor said with something between a laugh and a sob. "We're all dead. That's all."

"Why?" Nancy asked.

"I'll tell you why," Connor said to her. "Because this agent sounds like Andrei Bessmerkov, that's why. He's a Russian superagent, a legend. I've read his file on my dad's computer. No one knows what he looks like, but we do know he smokes a pipe with a unique tobacco blend. Before he'll let himself be found, he'll kill everyone on this ship!"

156

# Chapter

## Sixteen

NANCY WATCHED Connor's forehead tighten and his eyes narrow when he talked about the secret Russian operative Andrei Bessmerkov.

"He's a throwback," Connor said. "He's an agent who believes it's his patriotic duty to accomplish his assignment *and* kill as many American agents as possible. Man, we are in deep trouble."

Nancy looked away from Connor and noticed Frank motioning toward the door with his eyes.

"We'll be right back," Frank told Joe as he and Nancy stepped into the hallway.

Outside, the hall was empty except for a few stewards who were leaving newly shined shoes in front of cabin doors. Frank leaned against the wall and spoke quietly.

"What do you think about Connor?" he asked.

"I think he made all the wrong decisions, but I think he did it because of Marcy," Nancy said. "He seems to have really cared about her."

"You believe him?" Frank said. "You think he tried to stop her, and when he couldn't, he went along with it so she wouldn't get hurt? And you also think David, Gail, and Demetrios don't know anything?"

Nancy thought about everything Connor had said and nodded yes. "Do you?"

"Yeah. Just checking," Frank said. "But why's he trying to scare us with this Bessmerkov bit?"

"Look at his face," Nancy said. "I think *he's* scared."

"Really? Well, why isn't he scared of what the CIA is going to do to him?" Frank asked with a grim smile. "Of course, the CIA isn't going to be too crazy about *us* for getting involved either. They appreciate civilian interference about as much as a brain surgeon does."

"We'll deal with that in Miami. In the meantime, what do you want to do about Connor?" Nancy asked.

"I'm going to tell Captain Helgesen about Bessmerkov and suggest that he keep a twenty-four-hour watch on Connor, just to cover all bases. But I don't think Connor's a threat anymore. I mean, what's he going to do—jump ship?"

They walked back into the cabin. Neither Joe nor Connor seemed to have moved.

"Did you decide you believe me?" Connor asked with a confidence that twinkled for a moment but disappeared with his next question. "And will you let me help?"

"Meaning what?" Frank asked.

"Meaning, get the disks back," Connor said. *"Before* we dock in Miami. Because Bessmerkov will have to get those disks off the ship somehow—sneak them into someone's suitcase or a kid's toy or something. And eventually he'll go after those disks and kill to get them back. I don't think I could live with that."

Nancy, Frank, and Joe looked at one another. Find the disks, spot the spy, and watch your back at all times—it was a big assignment.

"We'll find him," Joe said. "And, yeah. You can help."

It was late, so they decided to head for their

cabins to get some sleep and start their search for Bessmerkov in the morning.

The next day they met with Connor again, this time in the secrecy of Cabin E 217. Connor's bodyguard waited outside.

"Agents like to think they're invisible, but they're not," Connor said, stirring his cup of coffee. "We've got to think of people who are always hanging around us. Maybe the person didn't even look at you, but he was always near."

"Someone who smokes a pipe," Nancy said. "And someone not too young?" She looked at Connor for confirmation, and he nodded.

"Well," Frank said thoughtfully, "somebody who comes to my mind as a candidate is Pete Porter. He's the ship's first mate, so he can move all over the ship without any trouble. Plus, he was on the Princess Deck at six A.M. that first morning."

"That's right. He's also been asking me a ton of questions about you, and even about me," Joe said.

"And he smokes a pipe," Nancy added. "But there's also Baron von Hoffman. He's certainly closer to the right age to be Bessmerkov, and he's around enough."

"That's true," said Frank, pulling his hand through his thick dark hair. "He was on deck with me when you went overboard, Joe."

"I remember you saying you were going to throw your camera overboard if the baron asked you any more questions, Frank," Nancy said with a smile.

"I saw him at the ruins too," Joe added.

"Then, there's Stefan Borkafsky," said Frank, his face a study in concentration. "He's been hanging around. You may not have noticed him. Nondescript sort of guy."

"That must be the fellow I saw in the hallway the night I met you for the swim, Frank," said Nancy. "He *is* always around—on the elevator, on stairways—"

"And then, there's that guy who always wears the black shirt," said Joe.

"The one with the endless supply of five-dollar bills?" Frank asked.

"Yeah, Jack Freeman," said Joe. "That guy's definitely a suspicious character as far as I'm concerned."

"That's true," Nancy mused. "I've heard he's always paying for gossip—five for passenger information, and ten for anything overheard at the captain's table."

"Okay. We have Pete Porter, Baron von Hoffman, Stefan Borkafsky, and Jack Freeman," Frank summed up. "Well, shall we divvy up the list?"

"How can I help?" asked Connor eagerly.

"You've got the easy assignment, Connor," Joe said with a smile. "Just stay here with your bodyguard and keep out of the way."

"Who's taking our number-one suspect—Pete Porter?" Frank asked.

"To tell the truth," Nancy said, "I think George ought to follow him. Of all of us, she's in the position to do it most naturally. I'll ask her."

"What do we do if we think we've found Bessmerkov?" Joe asked as they headed for the door.

"Just don't let him see that you know," was Connor's gloomy reply. "Not if you value your life."

Joe had been assigned to follow Jack Freeman, but somehow, over the course of the morning, things had turned around. Now Joe was running up a flight of metal stairs leading to the Crown Deck, and Freeman was huffing and puffing after him.

Freeman finally caught up to Joe and laid a meaty hand on his shoulder.

Joe spun around. "I said *keep* your money! I don't want it."

"You don't understand," Freeman said. "This twenty is for telling me *why* you were bird-dogging me this morning." He pulled out a fifty-dollar bill. "And this is for telling me who asked you to do it."

Joe just glared and took off, not looking behind him.

Freeman started moving again. "Okay, a hundred bucks!" he called, still chasing Joe.

Forget it, Joe thought. I knew hours ago that this jerk is no international spy. He ducked into a small upper-deck kitchen and cut through to the other side of the ship.

Meanwhile, Nancy was looking for Stefan Borkafsky, the man who had stared at her the night she found the corpse in the swimming pool. When she couldn't find him in any of the obvious public places, she decided to take a direct approach.

She knocked on his cabin door.

He opened the door and froze when he saw Nancy standing there. "You're the detective," Borkafsky said. He stuttered slightly, and odd sentences came out in his shy voice. "Why do you have to be after my brother?"

His brother? Maybe this *was* going some-where.

"Who is your brother?" Nancy asked. "Is he on the ship?"

"Chef Borka, of course," the man said. "A detective to not know is strange."

Hmmm, thought Nancy, remembering her encounter with Chef Borka in his cabin.

"Your brother wasn't very friendly," she said. "What is he hiding in his cabin?"

"Leave it with him," the little man pleaded. His eyes looked away from her. "Please. He'll die without it."

"I don't understand what you mean. You'll have to be more specific," Nancy said. "Why would he die?"

"I will tell you," the man said. "I will trust. It's diabetes ruining my brother's eyes. He might go blind. A blind chef cannot cook."

Stefan Borkafsky explained that Chef Borka hated the idea of anyone finding out about his disease and the medicines in his cabin. Stefan had come on this cruise to be sure his brother was well enough to continue the job.

"But why were you following me a few nights ago?" Nancy asked.

"I wasn't," said the short man. "I was going to ask you to leave him alone, but I got scared. Don't tell anyone his secrets, will you?"

You've done a favor for me, Nancy thought to herself, mentally crossing one name off the suspect list. "Of course I won't," she said. "I understand completely."

"I thank you for your kindness, miss," said Borkafsky.

Frank thought a long time about how to go about auditioning Baron von Hoffman in the role of spy. Finally he decided to put the baron to a simple test: Would he allow Frank to photograph him? Frank figured that if the baron were really Andrei Bessmerkov, he'd never allow himself to be photographed.

But after taking two rolls of film, forty-eight portraits of the baron and the baroness, Frank doubted that von Hoffman was his man. And, of course, the baron started in with the shutter-bug questions that drove Frank crazy. Frank was relieved when Connor showed up with a message that the captain wanted to see him.

"Does that guy smoke a pipe?" Connor asked Frank quietly as the two of them walked away from the baron.

"I've never seen him smoke anything," Frank answered.

"Oh, well," Connor said. "You'd better hurry. The captain said on the double."

As soon as Frank walked into Captain Helgesen's office, Mr. Robbins, the Texan who was the big winner from the blackjack game, jumped out of his seat.

*"That's* one of them!" Mr. Robbins said, pointing a finger at Frank. "He and the other one stole my five grand as sure as there are steers in Texas."

So Mr. Robbins was robbed last night. That didn't surprise Frank one bit.

"Joe was guarding your cabin, not staking it

out," Frank said. "Captain, we knew something was going to happen to this guy's money, and we asked him to put it in the safe."

The captain gave Mr. Robbins a polite but frosty smile and said, "Just tell us what happened."

"I was in the casino, winning all night," Mr. Robbins explained. "That pretty little blackjack dealer just kept dealing the cards, and I kept taking the chips away from her. But when I woke up this morning, my money was gone."

"I've got an idea," Frank said. Why hadn't he seen it before? The blackjack dealer was a woman—Wendy Larson.

"Captain," said Frank, "I think I can promise to have the case solved before the cruise is over. If you'll excuse me—" He quickly left to look for Joe, but he ran into Nancy first, walking by the Paradise Lounge.

"Stefan Borkafsky is definitely off the list," Nancy said after explaining what had happened. "And I ran into Joe. He came up empty too. What about you? Did you check out the baron?"

"He's not a definite yes or no. Still a question mark," Frank said. "But let's face it: Our list was just a starting point. Bessmerkov could be *anybody.*"

"I'm counting on George," Nancy said.

"She's been following Pete Porter around like a groupie. Maybe she'll get lucky, and he'll speak Russian to her or something."

Frank laughed. "Listen," he said. "Joe and I are going to have to back out of this Bessmerkov thing for a while. The captain is on my case about the cabin thief, and I do have a new lead to check out."

Frank told Nancy how he thought the thief could be working in the casino. That way the thief would know who had won big every night. "The only thing that doesn't fit," Frank finished up, "is Faith Whitman. She said she was in her cabin all night reading a mystery novel, not gambling in the casino. And nothing was stolen."

"Frank, I just remembered something." Nancy snapped her fingers. "That book Miss Whitman was reading—her red leather book-mark was only a page or two into the book. Maybe she's a slow reader—or maybe she wasn't in her cabin all night."

There was only one way to find out. A few minutes later Frank was knocking on Lillian Hallock and Faith Whitman's cabin.

"I'd like to speak to Miss Whitman," Frank said.

"Faith! Put on your ears! You've got a guest!" Miss Hallock said loudly.

Faith Whitman, in a pink jogging suit, stopped knitting and picked up her hearing aid.

"Miss Whitman," Frank said, "one of the dealers in the casino said that you left your room key in the casino."

"Oh, did I?" Faith asked in her sweet, patient voice. She looked in her purse and said, "No. I've got it."

Frank just sat there, looking at her, and all at once the old woman knew that he had tricked her. She stared angrily at him and then grinned sheepishly at her roommate.

"Faith!" Lillian Hallock sounded shocked. "Gambling? You know I disapprove."

"Were you in the casino the night your cabin was broken into?" Frank asked.

Faith didn't say anything at first. Then she said, "Sit down, Lillian, and keep your white pills ready. Yes, I was gambling that night, and I had a wonderful time. I won three thousand dollars."

"Were you playing blackjack, and was the money stolen later that night?" Frank asked.

She nodded. "Easy come, easy go," she said sadly.

"I'm sorry I tricked you, Miss Whitman," said Frank. "But if we're going to catch this thief, we've got to get at the truth."

\* \* \*

It was almost dinnertime when Frank went over what he had learned with Joe. They were sitting at the bar just outside the casino, talking quietly, keeping their eyes on the blackjack table across the room.

"I can't believe the thief is Wendy," Joe said, watching the pretty dealer shuffle and deal cards with quick grace.

"It's a beautiful setup," Frank said. "She knows exactly who to hit."

"So what do we do?" Joe said. "Set *her* up?"

"Something like that," Frank said. "I have an idea."

Just then Joe saw Jack Freeman motioning to him from the roulette wheel.

"I'll be right back," Joe said. "I've got to go have a 'little talk' with someone."

"Can I get you anything, Frank?" Rick the bartender asked, sauntering over.

"Just a soda," Frank said.

Rick disappeared for a minute to take care of the passengers first. The bar was getting more and more crowded. When he brought Frank's drink, he asked, "You seem disturbed, buddy. What's on your mind?"

Frank just smiled and sipped his drink. "Tastes bitter, Rick. Sure this isn't diet?"

"Must have the carbonation set up too high," Rick said. "I'll make an adjustment."

But in the next minute Frank had to make

an adjustment too—an adjustment to the room starting to spin. Voices echoed in his head, and the sounds felt as though they would break through his skull.

Before Frank knew what was happening, he was slipping off his barstool. As the horrified patrons watched, he fell to the floor—out cold!

# Chapter

---

## Seventeen

GEORGE FAYNE'S strong arms reached and pulled. The rowing machine in the gym stretched her legs and then her back. Its computer read-out screen was telling her how fast and how far she had rowed and how well the other boat in the simulated race was doing. But it couldn't tell her what she really wanted to know—what was in the mind of the silver-haired man two rowing machines down from her?

It was almost the dinner hour—George's least favorite time for a workout. But she knew that Pete Porter, the ship's first mate, always worked out at that time of day. In fact, after following him around for six hours, George knew a whole lot more about Pete Porter than she ever wanted to. What she *didn't* know was whether he also had a secret life—as Andrei Bessmerkov.

Finally he stopped rowing and climbed off the machine. He flipped a towel around his thick neck and sat down on a nearby bench. Leaning his forearms on his thighs, he breathed deeply.

"Win the race?" George asked, turning off her computer screen.

"Always," Pete said, wiping his dripping face with his towel. He caught George looking at the tattoo on the inside of his right biceps.

"Navy, right?" George asked, feeling his eyes watch her every move.

Pete said, "For a while." He didn't smile or stop staring at her. "Why the sudden interest? You haven't said two words to me all summer."

"Sorry," George murmured. "I was just being friendly." With that, she walked away as if he had hurt her feelings.

Just as she hoped, Pete was waiting for her outside the women's locker room.

"I didn't mean to be hostile in there," he said, buttoning the jacket of his white evening uniform. An unlit pipe with a white bowl was clamped in his teeth. "There's just a lot of snooping going on," Pete explained. "That photographer and busboy are into something, and your friend the detective is too. I guess if people know someone's snooping around, they wonder if it's about them."

"If they've got something to hide, I suppose," said George, meeting his eyes.

"Everybody has something to hide, honey. Even Santa Claus," Pete Porter said with a laugh. They started walking out of the gym. "Well, it's the last night before we dock. Are you ready for your Fancy Dress Ball?"

What do I have to do to get him to light his pipe, George wondered. Ask to smoke it myself?

"I guess so," George said, watching him finally take a silver lighter out of his pocket.

Then, before he lit his pipe, he asked, "Do you mind?"

Do I mind? George said to herself. I've been waiting all day to smell your tobacco!

"Oh, no—I love the smell of a pipe," George lied.

Bluish white clouds encircled them both as Pete lit up. George smelled a sweet smell.

"That's nice. Special tobacco?" She sniffed the air.

"Nah," he said, "it's just an ordinary blend. Why spend good money on something you're going to burn? One of these days I'm going to quit smoking, anyway."

George kept the smile on her face although she wanted to let it fall. She couldn't believe it. Pete Porter's tobacco was plain, ordinary tobacco, and he was probably just a plain, ordinary first mate. She'd wasted hours on him, when she could have been with David!

As she headed back to her cabin through an open lounge area, she wondered if everyone else had struck out too.

Frank Hardy felt as though he had swapped legs with a rubber doll. His feet were big and heavy, and they didn't work very well. His head didn't feel too good either.

"Just keep walking," a familiar voice said.

"Who are you?" Frank asked thickly.

"Oh, boy, you're really in bad shape, Frank," the voice replied. That's when Frank realized that his arm was around his brother's shoulder. Joe was holding him up and forcing him to walk up and down the deck.

"What happened?" Frank asked, feeling the sting of the wind on his face.

"Somebody sent you on a little trip to never-never land," Joe replied. "I saw you fall and ran right over. But keep walking now. You're starting to make sense."

"Oh, man—" Frank moaned. "I have a killer headache—"

"Big brother, there was more than cola in that drink I found in front of you. You've been out for an hour. Someone's on to us. Maybe they heard us talking."

"Who?" Frank asked as he began to walk shakily on his own.

"That's what I'm going to find out as soon as I get you into this chair." Joe helped his brother into a deck chair and felt his head.

"Okay, Bresson—you're going to live. But I want you to stay right here and keep breathing this fresh ocean air. I'll be back," said Joe. And before Frank could ask him where he was going, Joe was off.

"Frank? Hello? Anybody home?" Nancy said, knocking on the door to the ship's photography office and darkroom.

It was nine o'clock that night, and Nancy was worried. On the Princess and Palace decks, the gala Fancy Dress Ball was in full swing. Nancy had put on her silver evening gown, and silver shoes and jewelry, but she wished she could have been wearing her running clothes. There wasn't much time left before the ship docked in Miami, and she needed to work fast.

In the morning Bessmerkov would waltz off the ship. And, as Connor had pointed out, the Russian agent might plant the disks on an unsuspecting passenger, then murder that person to get the disks back!

Nancy had made one pass through the ballroom—just long enough to get covered with streamers and confetti—and then she went off, looking for Frank. By now she had expected him to be up to his elbows in photography chemicals. He had to have the cruise photos printed by morning for the passengers who had ordered them.

"Frank?"

She knocked again and then went in. Maybe he was in the darkroom and couldn't hear her. She was eager to talk with Frank—he was always full of good ideas. Besides, Nancy was curious to know how the gambling lead had worked out.

Nancy was in the photography office, which had a small darkroom just off it. "Frank?" she called out a third time. Her voice echoed slightly in the outer room, which was filled with tall metal filing cabinets. She turned on some of the lights.

Maybe he'll be here in a minute, she thought, looking around.

The outer office was like a scrapbook filled

with remembrances of the cruise. Contact sheets and developed pictures were stacked in piles everywhere, according to subject matter and day of the cruise. The walls, too, were covered with prints from all the high moments of the trip.

Nancy walked slowly past the picture gallery and toward the darkroom. At first she didn't see the large frameless mirror covering the darkroom door, and jumped at her own reflection. Then, since there was no warning light flashing above the darkroom door, she opened it.

More prints, more negatives, and the strong odor of photography chemicals. But no Frank.

Behind her the office door opened, not all the way, just a little.

It startled Nancy. "Frank?" she called out.

But no one answered.

"Frank," she said louder.

Still no one answered. So Nancy came out to take a look. As she left the darkroom, the outer door closed.

The studio was empty. Nancy opened the door and peeked out. The hallway was empty too. Just someone looking for pictures, probably, she told herself. But she had to admit to herself that it could have been Bessmerkov, for didn't he know every move she made?

She returned to the outer office.

"Hello, Andrei," Nancy said, turning around and scanning the room. But there was no one there. She was alone.

Now Nancy took a good look at all the photos on the walls—all the happy passengers of the S.S. *Duchess.*

Okay, which one of you is Bessmerkov, she wondered. I know you're up there somewhere. He had to be up there somewhere! But how could she find him?

Nancy stared and stared at the photos. There had to be a clue in them, somewhere— something that would give her the key to the mystery. But what? She could go through the photos forever, but unless she knew *exactly* what she was looking for, she'd never find her man.

Well, there was no time to wait for the Hardys. They were busy catching their thief. I'll just write Frank a note, she decided. Then she opened the middle drawer of the desk and almost cried out aloud.

There, glinting up at her in the dim light, was the gold cuff link! But why was it in Frank's drawer? She figured George must have asked him to keep it safe.

Of course! Nancy had forgotten all about the missing cuff link that no one had claimed.

After all that had happened since, she *knew* it had to be Bessmerkov's. That was why he didn't dare come forward to identify it.

Suddenly the adrenaline surged through Nancy. There wasn't a moment to waste. She wrote Frank a hurried note, tore all the photos from the wall, grabbed up all the piles of them from the desk, and ran back to her cabin.

The cuff link! She couldn't believe she'd been so blind. Bessmerkov didn't want it back because it proved he was somewhere he wasn't supposed to be—on deck, throwing Marcy Durbanville over the side of the ship.

As Nancy ran down the hallways, she clutched the precious photos and cuff link to her.

If Andrei Bessmerkov was wearing the cuff link the first night of the cruise, wasn't it possible that Frank took a photo of it sometime that first day?

That did eliminate most of the photos in her stack, but still, this was going to take hours—and a magnifying glass. She could unscrew the large lenses from her binoculars to use as magnifying glasses. And, after the dance, she could get George to help her go through the photos. But there wasn't much time. And they *had* to catch Bessmerkov.

If only Frank and Joe were there to help! Where in the world were they?

"Hey, here's one of you dancing with David," Nancy said to George later that night.

"Oh—" George said with a little smile, taking the photo from her friend and studying it carefully. "I think I'll keep that one." She tucked the photo in her dresser drawer and then went on.

They'd been at it for two hours without success. Frank had taken hundreds and hundreds of pictures.

"I haven't seen you and David together lately," Nancy said. "How're things going?"

George sighed. "He's been really weird to me since Cozumel," she said. "I think seeing the body really freaked him out."

"It freaked *all* of them out," added Nancy.

"Yeah, well, ever since then he's been kind of distant. And then I got busy helping you. You know, he hasn't even asked to see me after the cruise," she said.

"Oh, George," said Nancy, hugging her friend. "He'll come around. You'll see."

"And if he doesn't, I'll just have to get over him," George said.

Nancy was silent.

George whispered, "I fell really hard for the guy."

"Maybe it'll work out," said Nancy. "Thanks for helping me on this. It's very important."

"I know." George dried her eyes on her sleeve and went back to looking through photos.

So did Nancy. People suntanning, George teaching her aerobics classes, some kids making rude faces at Frank, couples posing with the comedian in the nightclub.

"This is crazy, Nancy," George said.

"I know."

Nancy picked up another photo and stared at it hard. Then she did a double take.

"George! Look! I just found the other gold cuff link!"

George leapt over to Nancy's side. "Who is it?" she cried excitedly.

"It's me, I'm afraid."

Both girls froze when they heard the voice. Baron von Hoffman!

"Please don't turn around. I'm holding a very large gun in my hands."

There was a moment of frozen silence. Then, in a split second, Nancy pushed George with one hand and flipped off the light switch with the other.

"Get down, George!" she shouted into the darkness.

*Ping!*

Nancy knew that sound all too well. A silencer!

"George!" Nancy shouted. "Are you okay?"

There was no answer—just deathly silence.

# Chapter

## Eighteen

J OE HARDY SAT at the bar, shaking his head. "Rick, I just can't believe it," he said. "Why would anybody want to put knockout drops in Frank's drink?"

"Beats me." Rick's casual shrug made Joe boil, but he couldn't afford to show how angry he was. Not now. Not here.

"Well, Rick—you put the drink in front of him. Who was sitting at the bar within reach? It was crowded, right?"

Rick eyed him suspiciously, then seemed to relax a bit. "Yeah, it was real crowded. Packed, in fact. Could've been anybody."

From where he was seated, Joe had a perfect view of the blackjack table in the casino. Wendy was a good dealer, and her table was popular. But no one was winning anything big tonight. Did she know that Joe was watching her? He couldn't tell.

"Say, Rick," he said when the bartender came over to him again. "What's the time?"

"Nearly ten," Rick answered. "What's your hurry?"

"I'm late," Joe said, climbing off the barstool. "Busing a special party in the captain's cabin. It's supposed to last till two—but I hope it won't go that late."

There. Now Rick knew he'd be out of the picture till two A.M. Would he and Wendy feel safe enough to strike?

Outside, Joe found Frank heading in the direction of the kitchen.

"Could we be wrong about this, Frank? If Rick didn't fix your drink, who did?" Joe said.

"I've been thinking about that," Frank said, "and I came up with only one name: Bessmerkov."

"Bessmerkov?" Joe supposed it was possible. Still, there was something about the bartender— Joe grabbed a croissant off a tray as they walked through the clattering, noisy kitchen and bit into it.

184

"Hey! Keep your hands to yourself and off my croissants!" yelled a chef.

"Government inspectors!" Joe yelled back. "How'd you like a citation for being flakier than your pastry?"

Frank shook his head disapprovingly, but he had to laugh.

"Come on, Frank," said his brother. "A man's got to eat." And so saying, he popped the rest of the croissant into his mouth.

They walked out of the kitchen and through another door leading into a dark, empty office. One wall of the room had large windows covered with drapes. And when the brothers looked through the drapes, they were looking down on the gambling casino.

"Sometimes they watch new dealers from up here," Joe said. "That's why the windows are one-way mirrored glass."

Frank looked down on Wendy, working her table below them.

"I'm betting that she's greedier than she is smart," Joe said.

An hour later an old woman wearing a black satin evening gown and a ruby necklace started winning. At first it was gradual. Wendy was giving a little, taking back a little, giving a little more. But after a while Frank and Joe could see that the woman had built a wall of five-, ten-, and twenty-dollar chips in front of her.

"Always an older person. They must sleep the soundest," Joe said. "Wendy probably knows her name by now."

"Later she'll look at a passenger list to find out the cabin number," Frank said.

Then the woman yawned and stood up. She was ready to turn in.

Frank and Joe snapped into action. They flew downstairs and posted themselves in a hallway outside the casino to wait for the woman in the black satin dress.

When she came, she was carrying her purse with both hands because it was heavy.

"Excuse me," Frank said. "Could we talk to you for a moment . . . ?"

A little later the elderly lady was sleeping peacefully in a different cabin, with her money tucked away in the safe. Meanwhile, back in her cabin, Frank Hardy was lying awake in her bed, with the lights out and the covers pulled up around him. Joe was ten feet away, hidden in the darkness behind a chair, ready to spring out when he had to.

The bedside clock with its bright digital readout clicked off twelve-thirty, and then one o'clock. Frank and Joe waited in silence, just in case Rick or Wendy were listening outside the room. The rolling of the water and the dull drone of the ship's engine were hypnotic.

A key in the door broke the spell. Slowly a crack of light from the hallway spread across the floor of the cabin as the door opened and a figure stepped in. As expected, the intruder was wearing a rubber vampire mask.

Slowly and carefully the thief closed the door and waited a minute before moving toward the dresser and sliding the top drawer open.

That's when Joe jumped out. "Tag! You're it!" he shouted, tackling the intruder around the legs.

The thief and Joe fell to the floor, grappling ferociously. Frank leapt to his brother's assistance, and between the two of them, they easily subdued the intruder. Then Frank flicked on the light and Joe ripped off the mask. Before them was Wendy Larson.

"Rick should have *poisoned* your drink!" she hissed at Frank.

"So Rick *is* in on this, eh?" Joe said. "Thanks for the confession. You know," he said as he turned to Frank, "I should always listen to my radar."

"Come on, Wendy, we're going to visit Captain Helgesen. I think he'll be very interested in what happened here tonight," said Frank, taking the blackjack dealer by the arm and pulling her to her feet.

"Wait a minute," Wendy pleaded. "I can give the money back, honest I can—"

"It's a little late for honesty," said Joe, opening the door.

"But it was all Rick's idea! I was just helping him!" Wendy had a wild look in her eyes. "He *made* me do it!"

Frank and Joe shot each other a look. They had heard this kind of self-serving talk on other cases. Wordlessly they made their way to the captain's bridge.

"Here's one of your thieves," Joe said, walking into the captain's office. "Her partner is behind the bar in the casino."

"I never wanted to steal from anybody!" Wendy cried. "You have to believe me! It was all Rick's idea."

"It was all Wendy's idea," Rick protested when Pete Porter hauled him into the captain's office. "She was the dealer. She set the passengers up so that they'd win big, and then we took turns breaking into their cabins. I never wanted to go along with it, but she kept at me until I finally broke down—"

The captain shook his head in disgust. "You two can consider yourselves under house arrest for the rest of this trip. The authorities will deal with you in Miami," the captain told them. "Now, get them out of my sight," he said to his first mate.

After the thieves were taken away, Helgesen's mood brightened. "Well, boys," he told the Hardy brothers, "I have to admit I had my doubts about your abilities during this trip, but I was all wrong. You've earned my complete respect and admiration. Let me thank both of you for a job well done!"

"Thanks, Captain," said Frank. "But we're not finished yet."

It was two in the morning by the time Frank and Joe headed for their cabins to get some rest.

"Should we call Nancy and tell her we nailed the cabin thief?" Joe asked.

"Why wake her?" Frank said. "She and George are probably asleep. We'll see them in the morning."

Nancy glanced at the clock. It was past two A.M. She and George were seated at the foot of one of the beds in their cabin. Opposite them was Baron von Hoffman.

"Baron—or should I call you Andrei?" Nancy asked.

"Whatever makes you most comfortable," he replied.

"I find your politeness entirely phony."

189

"Now, now, Miss Drew, I would like you to pass your last hours on this earth with some dignity. But perhaps you would rather that I describe in rapturous detail how much pleasure it will give me to murder both of you attractive young American troublemakers. You choose."

# Chapter

## Nineteen

So, WHAT SHALL IT BE?" asked Andrei Bessmerkov, sitting calmly with his pistol in his lap. "Pleasant chatter and phony politeness, or the naked truth?"

"Let's stick with the pleasant chatter," George said.

That made Bessmerkov smile. "I've actually become quite fond of you two during our little adventure together. Not fond enough to spare your lives, however. The enemy is still the enemy, no matter how young or pretty she may be. But I must admit, I feel I know you both very well."

With that, Bessmerkov stood up and removed an electronic listening device from the shade of one of the lamps. "I've heard all and known all, everything from your plans to search Connor's room to your little crush on David. Very touching, Miss Fayne. Though, I assure you, that relationship has no future—none at all."

George was so angry she almost charged him. "You're really a creep," she growled.

"Now, I must also admit that I have not handled this perfectly," Bessmerkov went on, ignoring her, "but I've never confronted such a talented amateur as Miss Drew. I assure you, had I assessed your talents properly, I would have put not one, but a dozen scorpions in your bed, my dear."

Nancy searched the spy's face with her blue eyes. He was obviously enjoying every moment of this little power game.

"How did you get on to Pipeline and her secrets to sell?" Nancy asked.

"Early on, early on. We intercepted the message Connor sent to that Central American embassy," Bessmerkov said, brushing lint off his sleeve. He checked his watch again. "We were curious to see the disks."

"Are they really worth killing four people for?" she asked.

"I assure you, I sleep very well at night.

192

Now, would you please remove your shoes and put those on?"

He pointed with his gun to their sneakers in the closet. George and Nancy were puzzled, but they did as they were told.

"Please tie the right and left sneakers together," he added. "Not too tightly. No, no, double-knot them. That's right."

"And where are the disks?" Nancy asked as she finished.

"They're safe," he replied with a little laugh.

"How did you kill Marcy?" Nancy asked. She hoped the longer she kept him talking, the longer she'd have to come up with a plan.

"You'll see." He laughed.

"And Julio?" Nancy asked.

"I went to his room and drugged him with chloroform, just as I did you in Cozumel. When he was unconscious, I put him into his bathing suit and took him for a midnight swim. He was quite alive when I threw him into the pool. Of course, I never expected you and your boyfriend to show up."

"Frank's not my boyfriend," Nancy said.

"Boyfriends are a thing of the past, anyway," Bessmerkov said with a shrug. "To finish the story," he continued, "after Julio saw the note from Connor on the crew's bulletin board, I knew it was time to act. I eliminated Julio and then sent the note to Connor to meet me at the ruins. Regrettably the police got to him before I did. However, the day wasn't wasted, as I did have the opportunity to drug you and leave you behind."

"Why waste a good outing?" George said dryly.

"Exactly," he said. "I'd hoped it would keep you out of my way for the remainder of the cruise. Ah, well. What else are you dying to know?" he asked with a sickening smile.

"You heard our plan to search Connor's cabin, and you beat me to it and stole the disks," Nancy said.

"Correct," said Bessmerkov.

"And you hit David," George added angrily.

"Lightly," he said, demonstrating with his walking stick.

"I'm sure your name will come up in the Nobel peace prize voting for showing such restraint," George said.

"By the way," he said, "I would like my cuff link back. I couldn't ask for it before, but I want it now. It was given to me by my Sophie. It has great sentimental value for me."

"How did you lose it?" Nancy said.

"I'm not sure," he said, a little distracted as he looked at his watch a third time. "Where did you find it?"

"On the Empress Deck," Nancy said, answering in a calm voice. Don't rock the boat, she told herself. Not yet.

"Ah, yes, that *was* a mistake," Bessmerkov said. "I should have claimed it then, but I didn't. I was afraid it had been found somewhere incriminating—like in Marcy's cabin." He looked off into space for a moment. "The Empress Deck—yes. That would have been the first evening at sea, when I took a little stroll to acquaint myself with the ship."

"Maybe you'd like to take a stroll now," Nancy said.

"You are a charming girl," Bessmerkov said. "I'm sure many people will have wonderful memories of you. Where is my cuff link?"

Nancy tried bluffing at first. "I don't have it," she said.

"You'll save someone's life by telling me," he said seriously. "If you could find me in a photograph, so could someone else. I won't allow that."

Nancy's bluff crumbled. She didn't want anyone else to die. But she wasn't ready to give up yet.

Taking the cuff link from her pocket, she threw it at his feet. Then, when he bent down to pick it up, she rushed at him.

But Bessmerkov was too fast for her. He twisted the handle of his walking stick and a shining steel blade shot out. "Its tip is poisoned," he said angrily, slicing Nancy's sleeve but missing her skin. "I know you had to try that, and I respect you for it. But it's time to go."

The three of them walked through the empty early-morning corridors of the ship. Walking wasn't really the right word—stumbling was more like it. With their sneakers tied together, the girls had no chance of escape.

Nancy couldn't believe how thorough and calm Bessmerkov was. He had left nothing to chance. Every step they took had been researched to make certain they would not pass a single human being.

But as they walked through darker halls, Nancy casually began plucking at the confetti that was still stuck in her hair and the folds of her gown. Every time Bessmerkov looked away, she put a few pieces away in the pockets of her gown.

They walked down many flights into the depths of the ship far below the passenger areas, where only specialized crew people worked. When they were nearing the bottom of the stairs, Nancy lost her balance. She slipped and caught herself on her hands.

"Keep walking," the spy said.

They walked on catwalks and through dark holding areas until they reached the fore of the ship.

"This lovely space is the anchor chain locker," Bessmerkov said when they had reached a heavy gray steel door. He pushed open the door. Inside, in a cavernous space, was a gigantic motorized winch, nearly one story high. Around it, glinting in the dim light of a single blue bulb, were coiled the enormous chains that were attached to the anchor.

"Bessmerkov?" asked a voice in the darkness.

"I have brought you two friends," Andrei said, pushing Nancy and George farther into the room. "They also have discovered who I am and must pay the penalty for that knowledge."

He took a flashlight from his pocket and shined it on a figure tied up in the corner. The girl was pale, gaunt, and wretched-looking, with dark hollow circles under her eyes. But Nancy had seen her before.

It was Marcy Durbanville! She was alive! But how? Nancy had heard of things like this happening. A drowned body is almost impossible to identify.

"Nancy, take those ropes," Bessmerkov said, shining his light on thick coiled ropes lying along the wall. "Please tie George and Marcy to the anchor chain. I will tie you, and I will check all the ropes you tied before I leave you."

"Why don't you just shoot us and get it over with?" Marcy shouted.

"Because I've never done it this way before," Bessmerkov said cheerfully. "Besides, it will be less traceable."

He cocked his gun and held it to Nancy's head. With trembling hands she led Marcy to a section of the chain near the floor and began to tie her to it.

"Who are you?" Marcy asked.

"A friend of your friends," Nancy said. "I've been looking for you."

"Marcy dear, tell them where you were when they were searching the ship," Bessmerkov ordered, a smug look in his eye.

"I was in his cabin. He drugged me and tied me up and put me in his bed," Marcy said. "He told the plumber I was his wife and that I was sick."

"Clever, no?" Bessmerkov laughed. "And the best part of it was when the body of an unidentified woman washed up at Cozumel. And to think, I actually had nothing to do with it!" He laughed uproariously.

"Where's Connor? Is he okay?" Marcy asked.

"He has a date with the CIA," George said.

"I really messed everything up." Marcy winced.

"Now, now. You did exactly what you set

out to do—you've embarrassed your father,"
Bessmerkov said.

"I didn't mean to get him killed!" Marcy
shouted.

"I think bigger than you do," the spy said
with a smile. "I've had a little more experi-
ence."

Once he made certain all three girls were
tied tightly, he pulled out his pipe and lit it.
The unique aroma filled the room. His pipe lit,
Bessmerkov turned off the flashlight and spoke
to them in the faint red glow.

"Ah, my first smoke in a week. What torture
it has been to abstain. And speaking of torture,
I am going to tell you the truth because the
truth may be less painful than your imagina-
tions.

"When we reach Miami, the ship will drop
anchor. When the chain is unrolled, the force
of it will knock you unconscious. So you will
not be awake when you slip beneath the water
with the diving anchor. I regret that I will not
be able to watch, but I look forward to seeing it
on the news. Ladies—adieu."

"You're scum, Bessmerkov!" Marcy yelled.
"You're lower than scum."

The three girls heard his footsteps and then
the door slammed.

Marcy cried hysterically.

"Don't give up; we still have a chance to

make it," Nancy told her and George. "When I slipped on the stairs, I dropped a handful of confetti. Frank and Joe will find it, and they'll realize no crew person would drop it way down here."

"You call that a chance?" Marcy moaned. "Come on, the odds are a million to one."

"Maybe you're right," said Nancy. "But they're the best odds we've got."

# Chapter

## Twenty

Frank... FIND US... *PLEASE!*

Eyeing the dim outline of the door, Nancy willed him to appear—it was their only chance. She, George, and Marcy had been tied up for hours, and every wave had carried them nearer to Miami. Once the dock was in sight, someone was going to switch on the motorized anchor, and it would be too late.

"Marcy, how did this happen?" Nancy asked, her blue eyes straining to see the other girl's face. "I know you met with Julio on the stairs, but what happened after that? How did you get here?"

Marcy let out a half sigh, half sob. "After I

met with Julio, a man came to my room. He said his name was Baron von Hoffman and that he would give me a lot more money for the information than Julio could. I didn't know who he was—or how he knew about me and Julio—but I had this crazy feeling about him. I couldn't help thinking that maybe, just maybe, I was talking to Andrei Bessmerkov. See, my dad had talked about Bessmerkov since I was a little girl—he was the one who always got away.

"Anyway, I told him no, and he gave me this cold, awful look. For some reason I just blurted out, 'You're Bessmerkov, aren't you?' I don't even know what made me say it. It was just a feeling I had.

"That's when he got really nasty. He pulled out a revolver, and I think he would have killed me then and there, except he didn't know where the disks were. That's the one thing I did right, leaving the disks with Connor. He's great at hiding things.

"Anyway," Marcy went on, "Bessmerkov made me go to his cabin. Then he chloroformed me. I think I must have been in there for a long time. I remember waking up and him coming at me with more chloroform. And I remember the plumber coming, and Bessmerkov giving me a shot of something. Then, one night he brought me here, and

I've been—" Marcy could hardly continue. "I never meant for it to turn out like this. Never!"

Nancy could hear George stifling an angry comment.

"You've been here how long?" Nancy asked Marcy.

"I don't know . . . days. He said, don't think of it as minutes and hours, think of it as the rest of my life."

A tense silence fell over the girls.

"My nose itches," George said miserably.

"Rub it on the chain," Nancy suggested.

"No, thanks," said George with a shiver.

The chain. It was swaying gently as the ship made its way toward port. How much time did they have left, Nancy wondered. An hour? Perhaps less?

I'm going to look up and see Frank at the door, Nancy told herself, forcing herself to think positively. "Frank is going to find that confetti. He's going to follow it down here. Then he's going to find us," she told her companions as convincingly as she could.

But even she was thrown off balance when the ship's horn let out a powerful blast and the winch motor roared into gear. That meant the ship was pulling for port even sooner than she had thought. The motor idled in neutral, making the anchor chains vibrate.

Nancy and George stretched their arms as far as they could so that they could hold hands. "You know something, Nancy?" George said. "These summer jobs can be a real drag."

"You're wonderful," Nancy told her brave friend with as much of a smile as she could manage. "I'm only sorry I got you involved in all this."

"Hey," George said with a shaky laugh, "it beats spending the summer sitting around the pool and watching Bess flirt."

"Liar," said Nancy affectionately.

The ship let out another long blast. This is it, thought Nancy. Once more she struggled with the rope that tied her, but it only rubbed her wrists raw.

At that moment the door to the chain locker banged open.

"There they are!" A masculine voice shot through the semidarkness. Frank Hardy was running toward them with Connor close behind him. But the chain was inching upward now, lifting the girls onto their toes.

"We're going to die!" Marcy began screaming. "We're all going to die!"

"Frank, *hurry!*" Nancy gasped. She felt her feet leaving the floor as Frank began tearing at the knotted rope.

"This army knife better do the job," he said tensely.

Frank sawed frantically at the rope with the small blade. Marcy's bonds were the first to give way. She fell to the floor, where she lay in a sobbing heap. Connor dropped to his knees by her side and cradled her in his arms.

Seconds later George was free too. But by now Nancy was dangling more than a foot off the floor. Her heart was hammering so hard she could barely breathe. "Frank—" she said, her voice cracking.

"Pull, Nancy!" he shouted. "The ropes are almost cut through. You can break loose!" He grabbed her around the waist and held her against the tug of the winch. "Come on, fight!"

Nancy thought her arms would come out of their sockets as she strained to break the frayed ropes. The winch engine whined as it labored against the extra resistance.

"Pull, Nancy!" George was screaming. "Pull!"

Suddenly Nancy felt the last strands of the rope give. She slid down into Frank's arms and he held her tightly. Then George was hugging them both, laughing and sobbing at the same time. Behind them the anchor chain made its way up and around the winch with a terrible grinding noise.

After a moment Nancy pushed herself shakily away. "There's still work to do, guys," she said in an urgent voice. "The baron is

Bessmerkov. We've got to stop him before he leaves the ship!''

Frank nodded. "Joe's at the gangplank. Passengers will be getting off in about five minutes," he said. "Can you run?"

Nancy was already halfway up the stairs. "Do you know how eager I am to get out of here?" she called back to him.

As they ran, Frank explained how he had found them. "Joe and Connor and I went to the photography studio. It was pretty obvious that the photos were missing. I thought maybe you had them, so we went to your cabin. Of course, when we saw the mess we figured you'd been kidnapped.

"I tried to think the way a killer would, and I decided to search the lowest part of the ship. It took a while, but when we finally found the confetti we knew we were on the right track. Joe's up on deck now, trying to delay the passengers from leaving."

When the daylight hit Nancy's eyes, it almost blinded her, but she kept running toward the gangplank. Passengers were going down one ramp and luggage down another. The deck was crowded with people milling about. Had the baron and baroness already gotten safely off the ship?

Nancy looked over the rail. There he was, casually strolling down the gangplank with his wife on his arm. There was no way they could get to him in time!

Suddenly she saw a familiar blond head by the top of the gangplank. Joe was standing with a bunch of other crew members, watching the passengers leave. Nancy ran over to a second mate, who was leaning against the railing, and grabbed the megaphone he used to give orders to the sailors.

"Joe Hardy!" Nancy shouted. "It's the baron. *He's* Bessmerkov! Stop him!"

# Chapter
## Twenty-One

ONLY A FEW PEOPLE near the top of the gangplank saw exactly what happened next. Joe nodded to Nancy, then went flying through the air and came down on the back of Baron von Hoffman.

The two of them rolled partway down the gangplank while passengers dodged to get out of the way and the baron's wife stared in horror.

Nancy watched as Bessmerkov got to his feet at the bottom of the ramp and raised his walking stick over his head. He started to bring it down on Joe.

But Joe stopped him just in time with a

quick kick in the chest. Bessmerkov doubled over for breath and fell onto his back. In an instant Joe pulled the walking stick out of the spy's hand.

In the act of pulling it away, he must have twisted it. To his surprise, the silver blade jumped out of its tip and stopped—one inch from Bessmerkov's neck.

That's when the agents appeared. They seemed to come from everywhere, swarming around Joe and Bessmerkov until Nancy couldn't see the two anymore. Pushing people aside, she flew down the gangplank to help.

She got there just in time to see the agents put the cuffs on Bessmerkov and his wife and lead them away.

"Joe! Are you all right?" she cried.

"Fine, Nancy," he said, looking with wonder at Bessmerkov's cane, which he still held in his hand.

"Hey, Baron!" he called after the prisoner. "Hope you had a pleasant cruise on the *Duchess*—it's been my pleasure to serve you!"

"You can go," the CIA chief told the stenographer. "The rest of this is off the record."

The chief sat down and cast a steely glance around the room. There sat Captain Helgesen, Nancy, George, the Hardys, and the five friends.

"Here's the good news, everyone. As far as I can tell, national security wasn't endangered during this little escapade. You're lucky.

"Nancy, Frank, Joe, and you, too, Ms. Fayne—congratulations. Your work was outstanding—courageous and effective. If you're ever considering a career in intelligence, please, come see us. You have everything it takes—brains and guts.

"Bagging Bessmerkov is one of the great intelligence coups of the decade, and you'll be well remembered for it."

He tensed a little and turned to the five friends, his face darkening. At first he looked at them without saying a word. Then he singled out Marcy and Connor. "Do you realize that you put a lot of lives in danger? That was incredibly stupid and selfish. No matter how badly you wanted to get back at someone, your personal desires aren't as important as the welfare of the American people. In this case, your judgment was worse than bad, it was criminal.

"Beyond that, you thought nothing of involving your three friends here in your little scheme. Did it ever occur to you that you were endangering their lives? No. All you thought of was yourselves."

Marcy and Connor looked down at the ground. "Sorry, everyone," said Marcy.